The Novel

Story by
SHAWN THORGERSEN

Based on the manga by
M. ALICE LeGROW

Art by
M. ALICE LeGROW

LIGHT NOVELS

A  Prose Novel

TOKYOPOP Inc.
5900 Wilshire Boulevard, Suite 2000
Los Angeles, CA 90036
www.TOKYOPOP.com

STORY	Shawn Thorgersen
ILLUSTRATIONS	M. Alice LeGrow
LAYOUT	Michael Paolilli
COVER AND INTERIOR DESIGN	Al-Insan Lashley
SENIOR EDITOR	Jenna Winterberg
EDITOR	Michelle Prather
PRE-PRODUCTION SUPERVISOR	Vince Rivera
DIGITAL IMAGING MANAGER	Chris Buford
ART DIRECTOR	Al-Insan Lashley
PRODUCTION SPECIALIST	Lucas Rivera
MANAGING EDITOR	Vy Nguyen
EDITOR-IN-CHIEF	Rob Tokar
PRESIDENT AND C.O.O.	John Parker
PUBLISHER	Mike Kiley
C.E.O. & CHIEF CREATIVE OFFICER	Stu Levy

Library of Congress Cataloging-in-Publication Data

Thorgersen, Shawn.
  Bizenghast : the novel / [story by] Shawn Thorgersen ;
[illustrations by] M. Alice LeGrow.
  p. cm.
  ISBN 978-1-4278-1030-4 (alk. paper)
  I. Title.
PS3620.H765B59 2008
813'.6--dc22
                                    2008016958

ISBN: 978-1-4278-1030-4

First TOKYOPOP printing: August 2008
10 9 8 7 6 5 4 3 2 1
Printed in the USA

Table of Contents

"I don't think they play at all fairly."
— Alice to the Cheshire Cat
(from *Alice's Adventures in Wonderland* by Lewis Carroll)

Dear Emma,

Enjoy the read, but above all things...

BEWARE THE GREEN CAT!

Very best,

Shaun

THE SICKNESS

*D*R. Morstan's stuff—Dinah couldn't remember the fancy name for it, though she knew the medication by its distinct taste of chalk dust—had been running its course through her ever since he'd arrived to treat her an hour or so earlier. Or maybe it was longer than that . . . the chalk stuff made time drip, drip along, as slow and strained as her heavy eyelids.

She lay in bed, her long curls splayed beneath her, dark rivers on the white shores of her aunt's linens. Outside her bedroom, the day had started: A cloudy morning had come to Bizenghast, the decrepit, all-but-forgotten mill town Dinah had called home since . . . how long had it been now? The doctor's stuff made it hard to think. . . . Biting her lip until she left small red marks, she focused as much as the prescription would allow. How long, she thought . . . how long had she been here?

The answer materialized through the mists of her clouded mind: She'd been in Bizenghast since . . . yes, that was it: since the sudden bursting of a tire.

That's how the newspaper reporter had described it: "the sudden bursting of a tire."

Right. She took a breath. The medication must have been weakening. More breathing and more thinking, that was the trick. Dinah tried to remember that old newspaper clipping.

She'd read it only once—after all, she'd been riding in the back of the car when the accident happened, so she didn't need an article to tell her about an incident that had left her bumped and bruised . . . and her mother and father far worse. It had been—yes, now she recalled—seven years had passed since the accident. She had been eight years old, and up until then, it had never occurred to her that sometimes, parents die and leave their children all alone.

Weak as it was, that chalk stuff, that liquid Morpheus, beckoned her to sleep—but if she forced her blue eyes to remain open, and if she kept her thoughts whirring, she could escape its lulling whisper. Sometimes, though, her mind raced ahead of her, revealing memories she'd prefer to forget. Memories, for instance, of that night in Drury, when she'd heard the tire rupture, sharp like a pistol shot, the screeching—she'd felt her mother's hand fire back to safeguard Dinah as the sedan's wheels screeched and the headlights set the double-yellow lines of the highway alight until oncoming high beams washed the whole view into blinding white light, a light that seemed like heaven—until Dinah had awakened later, here on earth once more.

As her mind cleared, she could see the newspaper clipping again. At the age of twelve, she'd found it in a shoebox under her aunt's bed: a jagged-edged strip cut with a shaking hand and blunt scissors. Dinah remembered hating the reporter; in six words he'd summarized the moment when her life had cracked in two. But the part of the clipping that had hit her, smacked her, dropped her to her knees—was this:

"*I just don't understand how it happened,*" said firefighter Neil Redmond. "*The busted tire we found was brand new with no defects or puncturing. It didn't even burst in a way you'd expect a tire would. It had a tiny puncture in it like a dart.*"

How interesting! How curious! What's more, the reporter had added: "Police are investigating the scene for signs of foul play."

Dinah sat up. A lock of her hair fell in her face. Her gown had crept up during her rest, so she tugged it down over her knees. *I'm awake*, she thought to herself. Most times, she just poured the chalk stuff down the drain, but whenever Dr. Morstan was here, he watched her take it. Now, though, she was coherent; the memory of that night—the shock, rush, crash so fast you can't scream—had snapped her into a semblance of focus.

Foul play? No. Dinah knew there had been no foul play, and she'd known it all the seven years since moving from her parents' home in Pennsylvania to this Massachusetts graveyard town. It hadn't been foul play or fate that had caused the accident. Forget fate.

It had been random chance. Chaos, if you like. Dumb luck. A cruddy roll of the die.

She took a final breath, flipped off the bedcovers, and ran across her bedroom floor. It was a wide expanse; her bedroom had been a convalescent chamber back when the property was St. Lyman's School for Boys. After the accident, her aunt had received the deed and moved from Colorado; she'd renovated the place to provide a home for her and Dinah, whom she placed in the healing room, as it came with a bathroom and was safely stationed on the first floor. In other words, it was the perfect spot for her newly inherited, troubled child.

Dinah sat by the phone and dialed, twining the black cord in her pale fingers; these days, with Aunt Jane keeping her from attending school or leaving home for the most part due to her "illness," Dinah rarely saw the sun. Through the thin walls (Dinah suspected that some of the renovations had been done on the cheap), she could hear Dr. Morstan talking to Aunt Jane. Most of it sounded like mumbles, but she pieced together a few words—words like "hospital" and "testing" and "for her safety." Now, she knew she'd beaten the medication. She was getting nervous again, which was partly what the stuff was supposed to prevent.

Likely, Aunt Jane hated having to assume responsibility for Dinah since the accident, and certainly believed there was something very wrong with her niece. Vincent, on the other hand . . .

Just when she thought she might get stuck talking to his voicemail, Vincent picked up. She listened to his breath; he was probably outside somewhere, perhaps riding the outskirts of town on his bicycle. His breath, and then his voice, soothed her. She knew so few people here—heck, there were only sixty-four residents in the whole town, including herself, Aunt Jane, and Vincent. Vincent struck Dinah as the closest she'd ever come to meeting an adventurer; he was brave, he liked to explore the abandoned homes in town, and—the bottom line was—when he came around, the *other* inhabitants of the former St. Lyman's school, the ones only Dinah could see, left her alone.

"Hello?" he said. She imagined Vincent standing on a hill somewhere, his blond hair glistening with sweat from bicycling, but light and long enough to blow in the chill wind. Possibly, he had some interesting gadgets in his pockets, ripped from one of the local buildings. That's how he looked when she'd met him two years ago. He'd been dared to explore the weird old Lyman's school, and he'd arrived with an antenna knotted to his bicycle and some crown molding strapped to his back, as a knight might have strapped his sword. Vincent had startled her, but perhaps she'd startled him, too; he'd discovered her filling what likely resembled a miniature grave in the yard. She'd felt certain she'd scared the boy away, but two weeks later, Vincent had returned with a discovered copy of *Le Petit Prince*, salvaged from some of the town's other ruins. Dinah was thirteen at the time; she couldn't have guessed that this boy might become her dearest companion.

"Come over," Dinah answered. She paused, listening through the thin wall separating her bedroom from the foyer. Sometimes, Dr. Morstan stopped in simply to drop off meds, or for a quick exchange of paperwork along with a brief update—not this time. "I need you here. Dr. Morstan hasn't left yet."

On the other end, Vincent took a deep breath. His breathing slowed. "What do you want me to do? He and your aunt hate me."

"But they know!" she said, and then her voice fell to a whisper. There was no way she could allow Aunt Jane or Dr. Morstan to hear this next part: "They know about the ghosts!"

"Don't worry. I'll make him leave. I'll tell him what he wants to hear."

"Please hurry." She felt helpless—like a fair maiden on a faded movie poster, grasping the brave hero as he valiantly shields her from black-hearted villains. She hated the feeling almost as much as she hated the chalk stuff, but what could she do? She had no power. No authority. And anyway, what difference would it make if she *did* try something? Random chance could happen along and ruin things anyway. Forget that. So, she might as well leave it to Vincent, who was much better at taking care of things than she was.

"Hurry up," she said, "before he sends me away!"

She hung up the phone and listened. They were quiet on the other side of the wall. Had they overheard her conversation? She sidled to the wall that separated her bedroom from the main hall and cupped her hand to eavesdrop, trying to imagine what they were doing in such silence. In her mind's eye, she saw Dr. Morstan, a pale, bespectacled man in his late thirties, sporting a goatee. Likely, he felt it was fashionable, but Dinah often wondered whether he was just attempting to look like a legitimate psychiatrist—a young, hip Freud, maybe. At Aunt Jane's request, he had been studying Dinah to ascertain the cause of her "fits," as he called them. Thus far, he'd discovered precious little—only that whatever had been troubling her through the years since her parents' passing and the move to her aunt's property often had left her screaming and bruised. He'd seen the fits himself, so any suspicion toward Aunt Jane had been quashed. He'd even tested her for the usual diagnosis, epilepsy, but that had come back negative. No, this was something else, and he hadn't figured it out yet, which is why Dr. Morstan had recently made his worst suggestion—that Dinah be removed to a hospital, where she could be better tested and treated.

When she'd heard that, she imagined towering white walls, wrinkled clothes reeking of bleach, and long, disinfected linoleum hallways spied through the reinforced glass square of solitary rooms. What an awful deal of the cards that would be, she thought. To be without parents was bad enough. To live in Bizenghast—which was, to her, the rotting cadaver of some colonist's dead vision—was to wilt alongside it. But to be alone, without even her aunt, or Vincent, her single friend, that would be the end for her. She'd never go to the hospital if she could help it, even if it meant somehow learning to cope with a house full of ghosts.

If only Dr. Morstan could see what she saw. If only he could see the Walkers on the lawn, the shapes within the shadows here in her aunt's home . . . if he could see the governess, the matron ghost that would discipline Dinah, and realize that the creaks in the ancient floorboards were *not* the damned house settling, then he would know everything he needed to, and she wouldn't have to go to some hospital.

But the truth was that only Dinah saw these things. And in moments like these, staring at cracks in spackled walls, the eight-year-old inside her, who had been happy before the sudden bursting of a tire, wondered whether the new Dinah actually saw ghosts, or was simply mad as a hatter.

"Hurry, Vincent," she whispered.

☽

The boy rode as quickly as he could, considering the chain on his bike sounded like it was going to rattle off and twirl around the rear wheel if he pedaled any faster over these dirt roads.

There, he saw it: the rusted, broken archway outside Dinah's home, informing any soul who came this way that this was St. Lyman's School for Boys. He'd always wanted to rip a chunk off that sign, partly as a souvenir, partly because a good hunk of iron presented so many possibilities. But this was Dinah's home, and even if her aunt didn't much like him, Vincent wasn't about to do wrong by Dinah.

He rode beneath the arch and past the brick walls, which were thick enough, he mused, to keep any of the old Lyman's boys from escaping, assuming the school still had a sturdy gate at the front (which it didn't). Vincent let his momentum take him the rest of the way, watching as the old school-turned-home grew large and looming, like a nightmare creature, in his vision. As was true of most of the buildings in town, Dinah's place needed work, and the boy wondered how long it would be before the ivy grew over the windows and covered the sharp rooftops.

Still, he loved his hometown of Bizenghast, and what some might label hopeless or strange, he called captivating, because you never knew how a thing might be if you fixed it up just right.

He could hear them talking about Dinah on the other side of the front door. Giving the bell-pull a good yank should hush up Aunt Jane, he figured, so he did just that. He grinned—she'd muttered something about killing him just as Dr. Morstan opened the door.

The doctor looked down his nose at Vincent the way some teachers did when they wanted to feel authoritative. Well, it wasn't going to work here. This doctor was a quack as far as Vincent was concerned, and even if he *did* know what he was doing, he was still hurting Dinah, and Vincent couldn't let that continue.

"Vincent," Dr. Morstan said, "what are you doing here?"

With as much innocence as he could muster, Vincent answered. "I came to see Dinah. Can I go inside?"

"Just a minute. Did Dinah . . ." At this, the doctor looked over his shoulder, glancing at Aunt Jane. "Has she had any fits lately?"

Fits? Vincent thought. Lying, he knew, was all about what you let stream through your head while speaking. To really, really get out a good lie, it was important to actually *think* along the lines of what you spoke. So, Vincent thought, *This doctor IS off his rocker, asking such a ridiculous and bizarre question* (which wasn't hard for him to do). "Sir?" he answered, as if completely shocked by the question. He nearly believed himself.

"Fits, Vincent. Has she been well?"

For an instant, Vincent faltered. Deceiving him, his mind returned to a scene not two days past, when he'd nearly had to wrestle Dinah down from whatever phantom force had been troubling her. She'd grabbed the canopy of her bed and held on for dear life, screaming loud enough that Aunt Jane could have heard from anywhere in the large house, had she been home.

When he finally brought his mind back to the present, he realized he might not be able to craft a good lie again.

"Vincent?"

"Um, she's fine. She's been just fine." *Dammit*, he thought. *I don't even believe me.*

And neither, evidently, did Dr. Morstan. "Truthfully, Vincent. Are you quite sure of that?"

Again, his memories ruined a perfectly good deception. He struggled to move past an image of holding Dinah; she'd been cold to the touch, deathly white, eyes flared open as though to absorb a giant, terrible secret. And as much as he'd tried, he couldn't pull her hands down from her face until her . . . well, until her fit had passed.

Vincent looked to Aunt Jane. She was youngish and attractive (for a thirty-something-year old, anyway), with brown hair, lighter than Dinah's, fashioned in a short bob. Her curled ends made her appear youthful, but the way she furled her eyebrows and pressed her lips while talking about Dinah aged her. Sometimes, Vincent pitied her, although she preferred he not come around. After all, she wasn't a mother, hadn't planned on being one, but was nonetheless put in a hard spot. Tough break.

That's it, he thought. He shifted his focus to thinking of her—to using sympathy as a grounding point for a little lie that could help Dinah. So, was he quite sure that Dinah was just fine? *Focus*, he thought. "Sure as I'm standing here, sir," he said, and left the spot a trifle too quickly to fully drive home the point. No matter, though: He'd gotten past Dinah's guardians, and that was the real objective. They weren't his biggest fans, but nothing he could have said was going to change that, anyway.

He paused in the hallway, waiting to see if they would follow him. Dr. Morstan spoke first: "Well, fits or no," he said to Aunt Jane, "those cuts and bruises didn't make themselves."

Aunt Jane answered, incredulous. "Are you suggesting *they* did it?"

"Come now, Jane . . . we both know there's no such thing as ghosts."

With that, Vincent walked the short hall to Dinah's room. *So*, he thought, *they wondered about it, too*. While sneaking around inside abandoned homes these last few years, he'd had his share of scares: floors that bottomed out, rooftops that caved, and the occasional shadow that looked remarkably like an old owner staring at him as he looted the place. But truthfully, he'd never seen a ghost—not that he'd mind it if he did. Dinah said she saw them, and who was he to disagree? It didn't much trouble him, because in the end, he alone could help ease Dinah's troubles, and that was the thing that mattered to Vincent.

He opened her door, and saw her—she was a year younger than he was, and she always dressed, well, differently than the girls in school; it was always something elaborate with Dinah. But his favorite thing, upon seeing her for the first time each day, was her eyes—her blue eyes, wide and sad, waiting for him to give her a hand. And he would—any day she needed him, he'd be there.

Dinah couldn't take her eyes off it: a baby deer—a fawn, she thought they were called—collapsed and dead on the trail. She stared into its large, deep brown eyes and wished she could have been there to help it.

"How awful," she said. "Must've been hit by car."

With Vincent's help, she'd escaped Dr. Morstan's visit by climbing out the bedroom window. That had led to sneaking along the brick wall and through a hole in the back of the property, followed by a trip through the trails Vincent knew so well. She needed the tour, the air, and especially a break from lying about in her bedroom, waiting for the next visit by the doctor—or worse.

Without thinking, she clasped her hands as though she were attending a funeral for the poor deer. "Should we tell someone?"

Vincent seemed less interested. Likely, she figured, he'd seen it before; he passed up and down these trails all the time. "Who would care? Let's go."

"Let's go the long way around, okay?" Dinah asked. The thought of returning home right after seeing a dead animal depressed her.

Vincent shook his head. "Uh-uh. It'll be too dark soon." As if to compromise, he added, "C'mon, you can ride on my bike."

She climbed aboard, sitting sidesaddle on the seat while Vincent stood on the pedals, the better to drive the chain under the double-load. "Go fast then," she said. "I hate the woods."

Vincent grinned. "I know you do."

They rode in the looming shadows of the woods. Above, the sun turned orange and then deep red as it sank behind the tree line. Occasionally, Dinah recognized a trail by signs: a fallen sapling here, a gathering of stones from an old stream bed there. She imagined that Vincent used signs like these as landmarks while touring his beloved town.

"These woods are so ugly," she said, calling over the crackling of leaves and sticks beneath the bicycle's wheels. "I wish they'd burn it all down."

"Too difficult . . . The whole town's surrounded by woods."

The front tire knocked into a stone, and Vincent almost lost control. Almost. Dinah figured he would regain command; that was what Vincent was good for.

He slowed the bike, which pressed her arms closer against his shoulders. "The way's getting too rocky here," he said. "We'll have to walk for a while."

Vincent kept the lead, pushing his bicycle as Dinah held him at the shoulder for comfort. The trees had started to lose their colors as the light faded; what was once brown bark and green leaf had melded into grim, graying silhouettes against a purple sky.

"Why do you hate these woods so much anyhow?" he asked.

Her hand on Vincent's shoulder, Dinah replied: "I hate them, and I hate Bizenghast."

She thought of the main square and some of the public buildings. "Remember when they were going to rebuild the old church? All the tourists were going to come back, and we would've been a living town again. But they talked and talked—and in the end, they didn't have enough money, not even for repairs."

It was true: She could accept that Bizenghast had the potential to be something greater, but the image she'd formed of it—of a rotting cadaver, the inhabitants its worms—had cemented the day the officials confirmed repairs wouldn't be taking place. They'd had the chance to resurrect the body, but they'd given it up, and now the body continued to decay—one brick, one cracked statue at a time.

Vincent nearly spoke, but Dinah hadn't quite finished. "Even that weeping fountain in the square bothers me. It hasn't worked for fifty years. Why is everything here broken? Why is everything so old and despairing?"

"You really feel that way?" he asked.

"I wish I'd never come here." Not, of course, that it mattered what she wished. All that mattered was random chance, dumb luck, a drawing of the short straw—

She heard Vincent gasp—if he was surprised by something, it couldn't be good.

"What's all this?"

They stood before a giant pile of—well, junk. But not just any junk, Dinah realized. *Old* junk. Antique junk. Old portrait frames, for starters, as well as gilded birdcages and leather-bound texts, their pages open and flustered in the soil. There were wall-mounted (now trail-mounted) clocks, mirrors, and wheels—and then the star of the show: one enormous, life-sized horse-drawn carriage (thankfully minus its horse and driver). All of this appeared to have been dropped from above, as if by a crane, although the surrounding woods were unblemished by tracks of any kind.

For a second, Dinah suspected that Vincent might've been playing a trick on her. After all, her friend did like to collect this kind of stuff . . . but really, how would he have brought it all here? Sure, some of it he could have carried or dragged, such as the old phonograph, or the chains and lines hanging from tree branches . . . but even then, what would've been the point of making such a big junk heap?

She turned to ask, but the expression on Vincent's face proved that he was as surprised as she was.

Vincent stepped forward, eyes taking in every detail. "What the hell?" he muttered. "This junk wasn't here this morning!" He turned to face Dinah, who'd absently picked up an empty picture frame and was looking through it, thereby becoming a work of art.

She watched him relax as he saw her. She hadn't meant to be lighthearted—she certainly wasn't feeling lighthearted about any of this—but at least they were together, and Vincent would still know what to do.

He walked around the periphery of the pile.

Sure, they could try to climb over the old relics, Dinah figured, but there was a pretty good chance of lodging a foot within some angled, unwieldy thing or another, or perhaps slipping into some rusted and jagged metal. Not worth it, as far as she was concerned—and she was glad to see that, by his expression, Vincent seemed to agree.

He turned back to her after scouting. "Come on," he said. "There's another path over here."

☾

By now, night had descended on the woods of Bizenghast—and with it, the cold. Dinah wrapped herself as tightly as she could within her old shawl, but she hadn't prepared to be out this late. The good news, at least, was that the clouds had cleared during their trip, and now a full moon shed silver light on the trail.

The trail had thinned some time ago—whether it had been a mile ago or two or five, she couldn't tell, but grass and dirt had at some point surrendered to dense copses of trees, brush, and thickets. One of the strangest parts of this trail (besides Vincent's apparent ignorance to its existence until now) was that, even now, some of the ropes and strings from above the junk pile would still brush against Dinah's face.

That caused Dinah to have a silly thought. It was almost too dumb to say, because Vincent would shrug it off as her being paranoid or something, but the strings and ropes above their trail kind of made her feel as if . . . as if she and Vincent were being led along. It was altogether too absurd to mention. After all, there were sixty-two other residents in Bizenghast besides Vincent and her, and Dinah *knew* Aunt Jane hadn't come up here—which left sixty-one other people who might have possibly dropped a giant pile of junk at some hour between this morning and now . . . and who actually cared to do something as weird as that to begin with. Considering that most Bizenghastians were retired geezers anyway, the idea became as absurd as—well, as your average ghost story (the fake ones, anyway).

The whole thing began to grate on her. "Vincent, there's no path here. Why aren't we home yet? I'm tired." As Dinah pulled one of the strings from her hair and waited for his response, he paused suddenly, nearly causing her to bump into him.

"Vincent?" she whispered.

She watched his shoulders rise and fall with each breath. Finally, he spoke: "What on Earth . . . ?"

Dinah stepped to his flank to share his vantage point. Below them, a huge clearing appeared in the woods, with crops of boulders marking a kind of trail toward an entrance between two enormous pillars.

Dinah tilted her head upward for a better look at the pillars; atop each was a sculpture of a kind of stylized horse. There were spines where the manes should've been, and they had exceedingly long legs, as though these fantasy creatures had traversed very deep waters.

Past those pillars, someone (forefathers of the town, perhaps?) had set gravestones in a borderless cemetery. Through this cemetery, the trail—now a formal, well-cut path—led to a statue of some kind, and ultimately to an enormous Gothic mausoleum . . . or at least what appeared to be the upper half of one, complete with sharp apexes, high, rounded arches, and flying buttresses to support the structure.

Suddenly, Dinah felt the *chill* come over her. That was the best way she could describe the feeling she had when ghosts were near. It felt as if she'd been laid on her back and dipped into cold, black water—but only the surface of her spine and the nape of her neck. That was enough, because then the cold crept through her, the way water climbs and darkens dipped cloth. Somewhere down there, things weren't right. Somewhere down there, she knew there were ghosts.

"Would you look at that? I wonder who built it . . . ?" Vincent could hardly take his eyes off the scene.

What did he think he'd find down there, she wondered. Trinkets? Riches? Or maybe Vincent's adventuring spirit called him to arms. Yes, that must've been it. She knew it, and she knew she had to stop him immediately, before he went rambling down the hill toward the graves. She clutched him and tried to meet his eyes, though his attention remained on the cemetery.

"Please!" she said. She was shivering now, and not from the cold. "I feel ghosts here! I want to go home now!"

Finally, ever calm, ever cool Vincent turned. "Dinah, there aren't any ghosts here. And if there were, you know I'd protect you from them, right?"

He would *try* to protect her. That was all she knew for certain.

As Vincent led, they walked past the two enormous pillars. Dinah felt the tingling chill and warily inspected the spiny equine twins. They stared at her wild-eyed, as though they'd stormed across these woods from some faraway land, over ocean and coral, one giant leg at a time, only to see this moment when Dinah would walk past and . . .

And what? What was this place, and why had she followed Vincent? Somewhere around here, there were ghosts. She *knew* it. So why follow? Yet she matched Vincent's every step, even as he tried to convince her that this graveyard was like any other. This was insane, she warned herself, but she couldn't bear to leave Vincent's side.

She looked up at one of the cemetery statues. It had been formed to resemble a robed woman blowing a horn. Her eyes, cut from marble, were blank and expressionless, but the artist had fashioned other parts of her from metal. The arm, for instance, complete with a joint at the elbow, held the horn in place, and her robes exposed a vacuous chest, complete with ribs, sternum, and spine.

Dinah had been to cemeteries before. She'd said farewell to her parents in one, in fact—but it had looked nothing like this. That cemetery had flowers, the occasional flag, and simple gravestones with the names of loved ones passed. There was sod, sky, and parking lots—as simple as that.

"These are the oddest headstones I've ever seen. . . ." Dinah breathed.

It was then that she and Vincent reached the end of the path.

"Um, Dinah?"

She saw it, too: the statue of the cross-legged angel, its face hidden under a finely carved hood, its wings draped in flowing cloth. It held a bowl in its lap, as though, despite its holy visage, it were a humble beggar resting in this unspoiled land. Behind the angel rose the columns of the giant mausoleum, and below . . . below the statue, Dinah saw . . .

An open door.

It led into earth and into black air. This, surely, was the end of their journey. Another step—one which would lead directly into that crypt—would be folly. She'd deserve whatever happened to her down there if she were crazy enough to actually descend into a pitch black tomb simply because it was there. Even someone like Vincent wouldn't be that crazy.

"Hey, let's check it out," she heard him say, eyes bright with curiosity.

"Vincent, no! We don't know what could be down there! Please, I—"

He turned to her. His expression had shifted to concern, but she could see him masking a yearning to know what waited within.

"Dinah," he said, "it's okay. I'll be with you the whole time."

So, this was one of those moments in life. At any moment, something was going to happen here, some flip of the Tarot, and her world would spin out of control once more—that much she knew. And the choices were simple enough: Refuse to enter and wait for him outside, under the moonlight, in the middle of a cemetery where statues had jointed limbs . . . or go with him. Either way, she feared that lurking spirits had a little something planned for her (and in the middle of a cemetery, surprises couldn't possibly be good).

As much as she hated it, she found herself stepping through the mausoleum doors, down into the black, into what certainly might be a tight, musty, confined space where hundred-year-

The Mausoleum

old skeletons lay atop granite slabs, jawbones stretched as if to say, "Really? Really, you've come to join us?"

That chill, that spirit sense, washed across her back and froze her fingertips as she held Vincent's hand through the dark—until suddenly the air cooled, and her breathing echoed the way it had when she'd shouted in her old school's auditorium, back when she could freely attend classes. The darkness gave way to soft, dim light . . . and soon she discovered the source: It was moonlight, somehow magnified, passing through the high, stained glass ceilings of wherever they had arrived.

"Well," Vincent whispered, "this is unexpected."

The place made no sense at all. Had they walked so far down into the dark as to allow for such high ceilings? It hadn't felt like a long descent, but this place disoriented her almost as much as Dr. Morstan's chalk stuff. As high as these vaulted arches were, how could they have been indiscernible from the surface? Giants could dance with the nobility of fairytale kingdoms here, in what looked to Dinah like a cross between a royal ballroom and a cathedral (minus the pews—the planked floors were free of furnishings).

They wandered the chamber, staring like tourists in a museum filled with gilded clocks and mirrors, ribbed ceilings, and doorless halls that led to who-knows-where, along with curving stairways at the far ends. Then, in the dim light, Dinah discovered something that didn't seem to fit here at all—a large black marking painted on the wall . . . graffiti, maybe. In front of that, the builders had fashioned a placard.

"Vincent, look there . . . what is that?" she asked, her voice echoing through the halls—swirling, repeating, and eventually dying down corridors she and Vincent had yet to explore.

The black symbol—which was nearly as long as Dinah was tall—couldn't have been designed by the people who'd created this place, could it have? Maybe someone else who'd discovered the area before them had painted this bit of graffiti, possibly even to highlight the placard. She studied the black markings and decided that the symbol looked like a six-legged bug with a spiraling tail on one end and an alarm clock head on the other. That pretty much described it. But what kind of people went around painting clock-headed bugs in buried mausoleums? Maybe, she thought, the same kind of weirdos who plopped heaps of junk on trails that conveniently conducted lost souls toward creepy places like this.

As Dinah leaned over for a closer inspection, she saw that the plaque had been inscribed. She read it aloud:

"In stone towers four,
Hooded watcher at the door,
And in alcoves threescore,
Let us be.
Behind glass walls we wait.
On our deeds meditate,
Until some luck or fate
Sets us free.
May you never try to find
What is hidden behind,

But if you're still of that mind,
Look and see.
To know what lies untold
In chambers grown cold,
Let each riddle unfold
To find each key."

Below the plaque, someone had mounted a single black key. It glittered even in the diffused moonlight, untarnished by dust or handling. Dinah's eyes were drawn to it; to her, it seemed the only clean and pure relic in this otherwise ancient crypt. She reached out and touched it, running her fingers along the cool metal as her voice still reverberated through the chamber, echoing the last lines of the poem.

Immediately, the wall behind the plaque divided, dissecting the clock-headed bug. Whatever device triggered the split, it was well maintained for such an old place; the shift happened so fast that Dinah felt her bangs flutter against her forehead, and she instinctively stepped backward for fear of what might've been unleashed.

Fortunately, there was nothing frightening behind the wall—only more writing. This time, Vincent read. "Lessee here . . ." He paused a moment before continuing. "Having entered the Sunken Mausoleum and activated this contract, the undersigned does hereby agree to be owned body and soul until such time as this Mausoleum's vaults are emptied of captive spirits or by the undersigned's sudden death, whichever comes first."

Then, Vincent's voice changed. He'd been quite the explorer until then, a regular heroic treasure-hunter, minus the whip and leather hat. Now, he spoke quietly, the way Dinah had heard people speak in hospitals to the very sick—or to the nearly dead.

"And here at the bottom," he gasped, "is *your* signature."

"No!" Dinah cried, disbelieving. Echoes mocked her throughout the Sunken Mausoleum. Had this been a trick? Or might this be the worst in a long line of life's cruel assaults? She ran toward the stairwell to escape, stopping short when she heard another metallic latch trigger above her.

A small, convex, brass hatch popped open, innocent as a cuckoo's hourly entrance—until she saw the darkness that had been trapped within. And in that darkness, Dinah could just make out a pair of narrowed white eyes . . .

Narrowed white eyes and legs—spidery legs, spilling like sprouts, like black petals peeling from a bud. Descending from the hole in the ceiling, the creature, whatever it was, moved swiftly, with a herky-jerky grace, the way people in film move when you crank the reel forward in double time. So many legs, each with curled talons—and spines running from angular shins, over knee joints, upward onto what appeared to be a kind of thigh. Yes, thighs . . . The bottom half of the creature seemed spider-like, or perhaps octopus-like (for it had a toothy maw on the underside), whereas the top of it—*she*—was humanoid from the torso up . . . humanoid, albeit with twin fangs hidden behind scarlet lips. Atop the monster's head (or as part of her head?) she bore a jester's cap, complete with bells that jingled.

The creature continued its descent from the ceiling until coming to a smooth halt in the air just above Dinah.

Before, Dinah had felt fear lapping against the base of her neck and spine, a chilly tingling that implied the presence of ghosts. Now, confronted by this creature, Dinah's gaze darted between the bestial maw and the needle fangs in its mouth, feeling as if she'd stumbled and fallen over a cliff wall into an ocean jingling and ringing with ice crystals, the water seeping into her ears, eyes, mouth . . .

This creature was a terror unlike any car accident, unlike any ghostly shade she'd watched glide past her bedroom door at night, her bedsheet linens pulled tightly beneath her eyelids. Here was a flesh-and-blood monster—capable, perhaps, of taking her skull in its maw and compressing until there came a crack, the spurting of fluid, and the loss of consciousness.

The blood rushed from Dinah's face. Her eyes stared; she lost the power to move them. Her mouth dropped loose, hanging agape. Her brain, grasping at any shred of memory or reason to resist breaking, conjured the image of hundred-year-old skeletons. *"Surprise, surprise,"* their open jaws seemed to say this time. *"Surprise, Dinah, today is the day you die."*

Before the creature dropped yet closer—her spider-limbs outstretched as if to snare the girl, pulling her struggling frame up, up into the darkness behind the latch—Dinah took in one more detail: On her chest, this creature bore the same clock-headed bug symbol Dinah had spied on the wall.

So, it hadn't been graffiti after all.

The creature raised her human arms and stared at Dinah, her half-moon eyes nearly as white as its porcelain skin. The grotesque creature's jester hat jingled; the muscles in her limbs pulled and thickened as each leg stretched and bent to some rhythm Dinah's breaking mind couldn't fathom.

"Hello, Dinah," said the spider to the fly. "We've been waiting for you for a very long time."

THE GILDED CAGE

*W*HERE had she been all this time? White light—seconds . . . minutes . . . hours ago . . . maybe yesterday?—white light had washed over Dinah's eyes, reminding her of the way her father cleaned the windshield at the gas station, of all things.

Suds sunk, sluggish and white, cutting sunlight, smearing the image of her father until he reached his arm across and wiped the glass clean.

White light . . . Was she in the car again?

Someone held her now, protecting her. She could feel arms around her, the arms of a guardian. Her mother? Yes. Her mother had pressed her hand hard against Dinah's chest to keep her in place, to try to save her daughter from the sudden bursting of a tire.

"Dinah!" she heard . . . it was a whisper, a boy's whisper.

Vincent. Vincent was here. *He* was holding her, not her mother.

Dinah had nearly fainted—and as the white now faded from her eyes, revealing her reality, she wished she *had* fainted: The monster was still there, bearing curved fangs beneath a claret grin . . . watching Dinah.

Vincent stepped to the front, shielding Dinah, who peeked at the creature over his shoulder while gripping Vincent's scarf with desperation. If this monster tried to take Dinah away into her ceiling recess, she would have to lift both Dinah and Vincent—and Vincent would fight to the bitter end, Dinah was sure of that.

Dinah saw now that the creature didn't hover as she'd initially believed—nor had the half-jester, half-arachnid descended on a spider's string. Rather, the monster seemed attached by cables implanted into her back. Whether the embedded connectors caused the creature pain, Dinah couldn't tell, for the beast betrayed nothing but pleasure as she ogled Dinah ceaselessly, not even interrupting her dreadful gaze when Vincent stepped forward. To Dinah's dismay, the monster seemed to care nothing for Vincent whatsoever.

The monstrosity spoke again, with the slightest impediment—a result of the soft pink insides of her lips rubbing against her ivory fangs. "Bali-Lali is so pleased to meet you, Dinah."

Awake again, Dinah swam in the ice ocean of fear, her senses all but fried. She struggled to keep from sinking into deep black, managing only five words: "Vincent, make it go away."

"Not going away anytime soon, Dinah," the creature answered.

At least, Dinah thought, this thing was speaking; she found comfort in that. Whatever it was, it didn't seem to want to eat her—yet. She struggled to push herself from behind Vincent, if only because this Bali-Lali seemed to take no notice of him at all.

"What do you want with us?"

"Dinah used the key and thus signed our contract. Dinah belongs to the Sunken Mausoleum now. Dinah is *owned*." The she-beast seemed to take some special glee in that—emphasized, in part, by the monster's sudden ascension toward the ceiling. Dinah watched the cables heave the beast upward as though Bali-Lali were a part of the Mausoleum itself . . . a puppet of sorts, maybe, or a twisted cuckoo.

"Those who are owned do our work for us. Then, they may go."

As Bali-Lai rose, gears squealed and cables moaned within the ceiling hatch, all part of a hidden, tortuous machine. Dinah thought she could see more white eyes staring at her up in the shadows, but she averted her gaze, worrying she might grow faint again if she accepted there were more creatures like this up in the ceiling or attic—or whatever that shadow space was. It was as if Dinah had walked in the center of an insect trap; the swarm crept and tapped on the thin walls, enticed, possibly, by the warmth of the living.

"Outside," Bali-Lali continued, "are the markers. Each riddle opens a marker. Each marker leads into a vault. In each vault is a spirit—some unhappy, some angry. All are sleeping. Solve their riddles and wake them up."

Bali-Lali had reached the ceiling. The creature slipped several legs into the hole; others she spread across the threshold for balance. "Help them wake peacefully. Send them on their way. Do not force them." Dinah heard the points of each spiderlike leg clattering against the ceiling. It sounded like fingernails tapping against classroom desks, or like the time a squirrel got trapped in the walls of her parents' home in Pennsylvania. (Dinah had thought the patter was a monster, but her mother had explained there was no such thing as monsters. . . .)

Bali-Lali

"Finish and leave before dawn . . . then, come back tomorrow night . . . and the next." Shadow crept up the creature's torso, a rising pool of ink, as the rest of Bali-Lali's spider limbs flexed and dipped into the hole. Her face seemed to glow, contrasting the dim light of the ceiling, until even that faded, and all that remained of Bali-Lali were two half-moon eyes, cold and eager as they had ever been.

The mechanics within the hatch whirred to life, and Bali-Lali whispered one more thing—"And bring me some gold!"—before the brass hatch slammed shut, effecting a metallic ring that echoed in the empty halls.

Dinah and Vincent were alone again, except for the fact that unseen monsters skittered in the ceilings—tick, tick, tick. Even so, within seconds, the unseen horde dispersed, and all was silent.

Vincent spoke first. "So . . . solve some riddles, wake some people up. Why should we?"

At that, the hatch burst open yet again, and Bali-Lali dropped to mere inches above Dinah, faster than gravity allowed. The jester's face distorted, and she opened her mouth so wide that Dinah thought flesh might slip off the creature's skull . . .

Which is exactly what did happen.

Bali-Lali hissed. "If you don't . . ." Her lips peeled like latex, stretching impossibly thin and gathering in loose folds at the base of a new head that emerged from the mouth. It was a horrific, death-pale representation of Dinah's head—that is, if Dinah had been found dead and withering in the Bizenghast woods.

Bali-Lali's thought was finished by the giant death head, which screamed, *"Dinah will die!"*

Vincent allowed Dinah some time to be quiet. For that, she was grateful. They hadn't spoken at all since Dinah had seen the image of how her own flesh would appear after her last breath. Some day, she realized, she'd take one final breath—maybe as an asthmatic wheeze, if she'd lived long enough (although she'd started to believe that was unlikely), maybe as a struggling gasp. She tried not to wonder about it much more than that.

Vincent and Dinah had left the Mausoleum peacefully. Now, they made their way through the cemetery, walking among the markers solemnly, as though they were there to bury the dead.

When she could, Dinah started to speak. "Vincent, can't we—?" She cut off her own thought. More than anything, she wanted to run home.

"No. Let's just get this over with."

She found one gravestone. At its base, the mason had carved an angel's visage. It was calm and quietly content, which was what attracted Dinah. There was no name on the headstone, only an inscription that read "Cagey."

Dinah read the script on the headstone aloud:

"For my heart and his body,
This house is a home.
With bones to protect him,

Never lead him to roam.
With sweet song to open,
These ribs as a door.
And let him have no home,
Near my heart evermore."

If Dinah had to free some kind of spirit here tonight, then this one certainly sounded sweet enough; after all, the riddle spoke of home and sweet songs. That couldn't be all that bad, could it?

She turned to Vincent. "Can we do this one first?"

As Vincent examined the poem, he tried to imagine what Dinah was feeling right then—fear . . . dread. . . . ? He wanted to communicate some words of comfort, but he could think of none. What exactly did one say to a friend who'd just learned she'd become the property of a mausoleum?

But Dinah wouldn't have to do this alone, Vincent had already made up his mind about that. He'd been the one to lead her along the path toward the figure they now stood before. For a moment, he felt a pang—of excitement? Yes, he had to admit that this was something extraordinary, an adventure beyond any he'd experienced while ransacking homes. More important, he finally knew that Dinah had been right all along: Ghosts did exist. Unknown, fantastical creatures existed. And as far as Vincent knew, he and Dinah were the only people in the world to know that for certain.

He turned his face away from Dinah to hide the smile that had crept upon his face. He cursed himself for daring to feel happiness right then, even as Dinah despaired—yet he couldn't help it. He felt happy, despite the surroundings and despite that Bali-Lali atrocity. It was a simple quiet joy, partially attributed to the knowledge that he'd become the only person Dinah could fully trust. He knew it was best to keep that emotion under wraps, though.

Dinah's voice broke off Vincent's thoughts: "I can feel that awful thing watching us."

"Just keep walking." Vincent knew that his momentary joy had been selfish. Dinah needed comforting, that was the important thing now.

He pondered the right thing to say. He couldn't promise that things would turn out okay—and by the looks of things, it wasn't even likely. Nor could he suggest that this journey would be easy. The truth was that he had no idea what was in store, and he'd be a fraud if he were to say otherwise.

"It won't hurt us if we do as it says," he finally uttered, referencing Bali-Lali as if by code. It hadn't been the warmest consolation, he knew, but at least Vincent believed his words to be truthful.

Soon, they arrived at a statue of a curly haired angel who was playing a flute. She was shorter than most of the other statues, only an inch or so taller than Vincent, and whoever made her had fashioned the angel's midsection not of stone but of metal, in the shape of a birdcage. The design of the cage wires looked not unlike the boning of a corset, curving to denote the angel's waist and hips.

Within the cage, a bird—a living bird, here in the cemetery, of all places—sat on a perch. Dinah leaned in to take a closer look at the little creature. To Dinah's surprise and pleasure, it was very much alert, its tiny, yellow-feathered body looking fluffy and fit enough. Maybe, Dinah thought, there was more to this place. Maybe people secretly met here . . . other people who knew about ghosts. Or maybe the ghosts themselves kept the bird alive. That seemed silly, but at least it warmed her.

Her strength returned as she watched the bird skitter back and forth on its perch, excited by the prospect of freedom, perhaps. Dinah had found something living here, and that made her circumstances more bearable—for now, at least.

Vincent studied the angel, pushing at its limbs and wings, seeking a lever or a button among the feathers.

As he worked, Dinah imagined Vincent and the angel as mismatched dancers, he floundering for the angel's hand, she graceful, statuesque, and unimpressed by his amateurish method. Such was life, Dinah nearly whispered. She grinned. More and more, she was returning to her senses. She could do this, she told herself. She could get through this mess and then return home to her bed.

The bird shuffled back and forth, nipping at the wires of its miniature prison . . . its *safe* prison. "Free me," it seemed to say. "I have been waiting for this."

As she watched the helpless creature, Dinah pondered a question. Which would be worse: knowing for certain that ghosts existed and being compelled to walk among them—or discovering that Dr. Morstan had been right all along, meaning she'd been loony tunes ever since the sudden bursting of a tire?

In other words, was it better to walk free, but risk experiencing all the terrible things that could happen in this frightening world—or to be safe and sound, albeit trapped inside a cage or a hospital room?

In Dinah's mind, the best choice—to live with her parents and obviate the question entirely—had been snatched from the table several years ago. She'd settled for the second best up to this point: simply running from hospitals and spider-legged ladies with haste. One or the other would catch her eventually, though; this she was sure of.

Still . . . to look at this bird . . . Dinah knew in her heart it wanted freedom. She tried to open the cage, but it was locked and sealed tight. *I guess it's stuck inside*, she thought to herself. There was no choice for it, after all. The bird's longings meant nothing to the bird's caretakers, whomever they were.

"There has to be a key, some way to open it," Vincent said.

Hearing his voice brought Dinah back to the task at hand. "Her ribcage is a birdcage," she said. "That's so weird. What did the riddle say? 'With sweet song to open these ribs as a door . . . and let him have no home, near my heart evermore.'"

Vincent mumbled the riddle to himself before suddenly bringing his lips to the angel's face. For an instant, Dinah thought he might try to kiss the statue—but instead, he shared its flute, directing a puff of his breath over the mouthpiece.

To Dinah's surprise, the flute played a note! And to their mutual wonder, the bird fluttered its wings and joyously matched the note in song, which triggered a trapdoor in the ground ahead of them. Dinah turned back to the bird. It cocked its head backward and forward before tilting it as if to suggest it were as curious about Dinah as she was about the bird. She thought it seemed happy, as if it had fulfilled its role here. Now it could sing, even if it was still caged.

The trapdoor led into—surprise, surprise, Dinah thought—a deep, dark pit with no apparent bottom. Terrific. Thankfully, it came complete with a ladder. That was something, at least.

Vincent climbed on first, the ladder rungs clanking with each new step.

After Vincent had made enough headway, Dinah climbed on as well. She soon realized that Vincent was much better dressed for this adventure than she was. Knowing that Vincent's eyes were mere feet below, she tried to wedge her dress between her knees as she descended the ladder—but it wouldn't work. And she needed her hands for the ladder. "Don't you dare look up, Vincent," she warned.

For his part, Vincent had been too busy making sure he wasn't dropping into some beast's gaping mouth to notice her predicament, but he smiled nonetheless. That she worried about giving him a show meant she was coping in his mind's eye. With that issue out of the way, he could shift his focus to the next problem: how to avoid looking up now that his attention had been called to certain circumstances.

The ladder ended in a simple chamber, the only notable detail being a single door fashioned with a simple brass handle. Vincent found the door curious; unlike the doors in his home or those he'd seen on his raids through abandoned houses in Bizenghast, this door seemed to be made of the same material as the walls. For that matter, it seemed to *be* part of the wall, delineated only by a thin, arching edge and tiny hinges. If not for the handle, he might have missed the door at first inspection, mistaking it for another wall.

Once Dinah reached the base and joined him, Vincent reached for the handle. This was it, he knew it: Behind this strange door, the first adventure awaited. It felt to him like he should say something meaningful, something profound; after all, this was like taking the first step on the moon or sailing across some uncharted waters.

"I wonder what ghosts dream about," he said.

Dinah watched the muscles in his hand pull as he tugged at the door. "I don't want to know," she replied.

And with that, they stepped through the portal, feeling the rush of traveling through—what? Time? Space? Another psyche?

The floor had dropped from beneath their feet, and Vincent could feel air blasting through his blond hair, so he supposed they must be traveling through some kind of space—and quickly, at that. Down, over, or through they went, until they stopped, now on the other side of the door that resembled a wall.

Vincent rubbed his eyes and gave himself a moment to get over the sensation of having fallen into this realm. When his vision cleared, he saw that they were both standing under a stone arch. He guessed that it was the equivalent of the doorway on this side of the portal. Passing back through the arch seemed to have no effect, though; it certainly didn't return him to the underground chamber. Evidently, the journey between thresholds was one way only. However they were expected to return to their own time and place, it wouldn't be by simply walking back through the archway.

They'd appeared outside, under overcast skies. Ahead of them, at a distance of no more than twenty yards across overgrown grass, the earth itself was devouring a crumbling plantation manor, one stone at a time. Ingestion would take years by the look of it, but the fallow land seemed to favor one side over the other, so the home sat on a steep angle, its attached patio apparently the tastiest of its parts.

Trees festooned with witch's hazel grew upon the roof of the manor, and here and there the property itself bore craggy crevasses, like gashes cut with a giant's dagger. To complete the image, peculiar networks of cable ran along the wounds, reminiscent of bones and tendons—or, more pertinent, of the cords that connected Bali-Lali to the Mausoleum. Maybe, Vincent thought, this ghost's world is breaking down, and creatures like Bali-Lali came to keep the realm from disintegrating. It was nothing more than a theory, of course, but as Vincent walked toward the home, he wondered whether he and Dinah had arrived just in time to set things right.

As they neared, a vase crashed through a first-floor window. Somewhere inside, a girl screamed, "Keep away!" and Vincent thought he heard two sets of footsteps—one light and swift, the other determined and plodding.

"Hear that?" he asked Dinah. "Someone's in trouble! Come on!" He was about to rush to the front door—and break it down if need be—when Dinah answered.

"No, I can't go in there, Vincent!"

He wanted to stay by her side, but someone was in danger—and wasn't the whole point of this excursion to save some soul, anyway? The way he figured it, he could best help Dinah by rescuing this soul, or whatever he would find in there. That way, maybe they could return safely to their own world again.

"Dinah, it's okay. I'll go. You wait here." Her name might be on the contract, but he was here with her, and he doubted it mattered much who solved this situation as long as it got solved.

He ran. By the time he reached the front door, he could hear Dinah sobbing, and it was all he could do not to turn around. *This is how I can help her*, he assured himself, *by taking care of things for her.* He tried to ignore the other part of him, the adventurer, who was eager to break into the manor simply to see what was what. This was about Dinah, after all.

"Stay back! Stop it!" the mysterious girl screamed again. Vincent had no idea who she could be, or what condition she might be in once he found her. He wasn't even sure whether she'd look human—after all, wasn't she supposed to be dead? All he knew for sure was that her voice issued from one window and then another as she desperately fled some unidentified threat.

Vincent would try entering the manor the proper way first: He banged on the door, calling, "Hey, open up in there! Open the door!"

No use. He'd already guessed that wasn't going to work. That's why he didn't mind shifting to plan B, which involved a good kick to an adjacent window. He'd had plenty of practice breaking into abandoned homes back in Bizenghast to scavenger, so he was inside with barely more than a scratch on his cheek, having first knocked out the remaining shards and then clambered in using his gloves and scarf for protection.

Once his feet touched the floor, he heard the mysterious girl call out again: "Poppy, please! Get away!"

Just then, the source of the fracas ran across the hall: a blonde-haired girl about Vincent's age, lovely in her petticoat—except for the expression of terror on her face. Oddly, her waist was open, and this girl spirit had no flesh or bone from beneath her ribs to the tops of her hips. Instead, birdcage wires connected her top and bottom. And like the "Cagey" statue back at the Mausoleum, the girl had a bird fluttering about inside her wired midsection.

So, Vincent thought, *ghosts aren't always going to look like they did in life*. He wondered whether they could be touched, or whether this girl only *looked* real to him. His darker imagination went so far as to wonder whether a set of pliers could cut this ghost's wiry midsection in two, thus dividing her figure. It was a silly question, and a time-wasting one at that, yet Vincent's stream of conscience continued unchecked as he turned his focus to Dinah; surely, his friend wouldn't be frightened by Cagey's abstract form, but what if others were twisted in more terrifying ways?

He had little more time for that line of thought to continue, though, as Vincent had discovered who had been chasing the girl: her would-be killer, an older man whose long gray ponytail wavered behind him as he gave chase with a double-headed ax in hand.

"No, Poppy! Please!" the girl shouted again.

With little opportunity to wonder why this man would want to kill his granddaughter, Vincent dashed between the hunter and the hunted, yelling, "Hold it!"

Using the advantage of surprise, he engaged Poppy, grabbing the ax handle near the blades. Although the old man was mighty enough to heft the weapon and had maintained enough stamina to chase a child through the house, Vincent was able to prevent any attacks by grabbing the top of the weapon between the blades and leveraging his advantage.

So, he'd hampered the deranged old man. Now what?

The boy saw nothing but wrath in the elder man's eyes. This man saw red, Vincent realized. There could be no peace here, and if Vincent were to lose his grip, Poppy would not hesitate to turn the ax against him before continuing his chase. So, there were no options.

Even now, Poppy shoved at the weapon, baring his teeth as a hound would its fangs. No words would work here. This man wanted blood on the walls, blood seeping between the floorboards.

Very well, Vincent decided. But it wasn't going to be Cagey's blood, nor would it be his own. Focusing his youthful might, he pressed the larger of the two blades down so that it bit into the old man's chest, deep enough that Vincent felt weak resistance from the collarbone.

The cut, deep and leaking as it was, barely staggered the girl's grandfather.

How could that be? Vincent wondered. *Is he a ghost, too? And if so, how do you kill a ghost?* Somehow, before entering the next vault, he and Dinah needed to find some answers—but for now, Vincent simply grabbed Cagey by the wrist (he could touch this ghost after all), shouting, "Come on!" Already, he saw her grandpa recovering, so he escorted her to the nearest place he could find, which turned out to be the stairwell. *Good enough*, Vincent thought. *Plenty of places up there to hide her and buy some time.*

They ran up the curving stairs, past carved angels perched on posts and, where the stairs turned for the final ascent to the second floor, up to an impressive window set. For a moment, Vincent released Cagey and ran to it, hoping to find Dinah outside, safe and sound. He'd left her near the archway, and he expected to spot her there now, still weeping—but this room was on the opposite side of the property, and he neither saw nor heard anything from Dinah. *Not good*, he thought. Hopefully, she'd merely decided to wait for him by the arch, or possibly by the manor's front door. But what if she'd decided to enter after him? No, he wouldn't even think about that possibility, because Vincent knew he couldn't protect both Dinah and this girl from an undying, enraged man with an ax. Dinah was fine, he assured himself, none too convincingly.

☽

How much time had passed, Dinah couldn't tell. Did time even pass in this place at all? All she knew was that Vincent had broken into the place, and that the last she'd heard from him was a shout—"Hold on!" or something like that. There had been no sound afterward beyond the crash of decorations within.

Thank goodness he's here, she thought. *I couldn't—how could I possibly be of use in this place?* And what would she ever do if something happened to Vincent, leaving her alone?

She covered her eyes and wept again, half ashamed of herself, half terrified that any moment Vincent might stumble out mortally wounded. Then, she heard footfalls on the grass, light and swift. Could it be? Had Vincent already returned?

What approached was nothing like Vincent. They weren't even human. Two creatures—doglike, except their jaws were upside down—were ambling toward her. A long strip of drool dangled from the alpha dog's lower (that is, *upper*) jaw.

Dinah knew at once these creatures hadn't approached out of curiosity. They were here to devour her. These were bulky, tough creatures, built for sprinting short distances toward prey. They no doubt used their weight to pin down hapless creatures until one of their pack could dig its incisors deep into the throat, tearing out the jugular.

Now, their brawny front legs shoved against the grass as the creatures flung themsleves forward toward Dinah, barking to signal the commencement of the hunt.

Dinah quickly estimated that she had fifteen feet or so on the creatures as she frantically searched for a hiding spot. She couldn't possibly make it as far as the house before they reached her; these creatures were too swift, driven as they were by hunger. Instead, she turned back to the archway, leaping as high as she could and reaching her fingers around the top edge of the structure. Her fingers scraped against the stone as bits of mortar dropped from the archway into her hair and eyes. She cried out for Vincent, hoping that he might hear, returning to save her.

Beneath her, the creatures jumped and snatched at her skirt, tearing off shreds and then shaking the cloth pieces as if they hoped to find some morsel of flesh ripped from Dinah's calves. They were so eager that Dinah feared she'd lost some of herself to the creatures already, and that her own shock was preventing her from registering the agony of hewn skin and tissue.

Using all her might, Dinah scrambled to the top of the arch, swinging her legs over the edge. Below, the dog things leapt and bit at the air, growling and whining in frustration.

Settled safely now, Dinah checked herself for wounds, finding none. She'd been lucky. Feeling sorry for herself had nearly cost her life. Moreover, her fear had separated her from Vincent, which meant that this mission—and her fate—was now entirely in his hands.

Once Cagey spoke up, Vincent was able to dismiss his worries about Dinah and return his attention to the matter at hand. The girl had a soothing voice, Vincent noted, at least when she wasn't using it to utter larynx-ripping screams.

"My grandfather's gone starkers. . . . He says I'm a demon! He's had me trapped in the house for months!"

In the moment, it barely occurred to Vincent that he was talking to an actual ghost; his focus was set on finding a way to rescue this girl spirit and return to Dinah. "It's okay now.

Follow me!" he said (though where exactly he would lead her in her own house, he had no idea).

From somewhere downstairs, Vincent heard the ax clatter to the floor. Whatever the old man had planned next, he wouldn't be wielding the blade—but since the goal surely remained cold-blooded, maniacal murder, the new strategy couldn't be good, ax or no ax.

The run upstairs brought Vincent to a door that opened upon the exterior of the house—to the rotting, overgrown roof. Here, he could see the trees that flourished upon the house, their roots insinuating themselves between shingles and ultimately, perhaps, somewhere within the manor's crawlspaces.

He looked for a weapon, a branch maybe, among the flora. Nothing. These were living trees, improbable as they were, and their twisting bark hadn't surrendered to disease or the elements. Up here, of all places, life bloomed and invaded the short-lived fabrications of man, no patch of cement or brick went evading vinery or thick, furry moss.

Vincent heard the grandfather's footsteps clomping up the wooden stairs that led to the rooftop landscape. It reminded him of a game his father had played when Vincent was very young: His father would creep up the stairs to their second floor, where young Vincent would hide under his covers. *"Vincent, I'm on the first step,"* his father would whisper, the stair squeaking under his shifting weight. *"Vincent, I'm on the second step. . . ."*

Back in the present, Vincent turned to Cagey for help, but she seemed bewildered, as though she'd never been up here in all her years. "We're on . . . the roof?" she whispered.

Vincent expected to see her shiver, but she did not. Her grandfather was on his way up to kill them, yet she couldn't take her eyes off the trees and open sky beyond. She might be close to destruction, but she was also—

"I think I get what Bali-Lali was talking about," Vincent thought aloud.

He turned and saw Poppy in the doorway, this time holding a gun with a flared opening like a trumpet's bell. Vincent's own father had picked up something like that during one of his many travels to foreign lands. It was an elephant gun, Vincent recalled, termed as such because this weapon could be used to fell enormous beasts. He tried not to wonder what a blast would do to kids like Cagey and him, but he couldn't help but imagine that it would leave the duo without faces at the least.

"Vincent, I'm at your door. . . ."

His job—well, his *and* Dinah's mission—was to set ghosts free. This girl needed to be free; the fact that she marveled at this miniature forest assured Vincent that he was right. But how, exactly, was he to set her free?

The birdcage in her midsection . . . Maybe, he thought, Cagey was the trapped bird within rather than the girl herself! Release the bird, and the soul would be free from her grandfather. . . .

Reaching for the girl's abdomen felt somewhat brazen (to both of them), but Vincent had no time for polite etiquette. The door of the birdcage was positioned in the area where the girl's belly button would have been when the girl had walked among the living, however long ago that was. Vincent tried to unlatch it, but the door was locked.

Come on, he thought. As he said that, Vincent heard Poppy's shoes crushing the carpet of rooftop moss. With a quick glance upward, Vincent took in the old man's blood-drenched coat—and to his dismay, Vincent also discovered that Poppy had complete use of the arm he'd injured earlier.

Vincent heard the old man's fingernails scraping against the elephant gun. Soon, there would be a flash and a blast to set the birds flying from the trees and—

Wait a minute, he thought. *Birds flying from the trees . . .*

Trying to unlock the door to the girl's cage was useless. He pulled on it, yet the door simply would not open, as if Cagey were too frightened to allow herself freedom. But if he waited for her to be ready, they'd both be shot. There was simply no time.

The old man clicked the hammer into place.

Lifting Cagey into his arms, Vincent began sprinting toward the far end of the roof, praying he was right about this next move.

"It's time for you to be free, Cagey," he said. And with that, he dropped her over the edge of the roof.

Time slowed for Vincent as he watched the girl fall. For the first twenty feet, he feared the worst—that in an effort to save the spirit, he'd destroyed her. He'd hoped she might free herself if the opportunity were forced upon her. Instead, she simply fell over the side of the manor, her blonde hair flapping in the downward gusts.

Then, Vincent saw her eyes change from fearful to peaceful, and suddenly the birdcage door at her midsection swung open of its own accord. The bird stretched its wings and sang as it escaped its prison, even as the girl's body crashed upon the lawn.

The bird ascended, reaching the elevation of the roof, where it transformed into the refined, liberated spirit of Cagey. Now she appeared angelic, with a joyful grin that Vincent watched as the girl flew toward the treetops, clouds, and sun before finally disappearing in the light.

Great! Vincent thought. *I've done it!*

But when he heard the old man hiss at the loss of his granddaughter, Vincent turned and found himself facing the business end of the firearm, which was pointed directly at his face.

The old man pulled the trigger, and once again time seemed to slow. Vincent watched a plume of smoke curl and cloud over the weapon. He heard thunder and saw the shot coming directly for him.

This is it, he thought. *So, how's this work? If I die in a ghost's dream, where's that put me?*

There was a flash of light. He lost his vision and his body numbed.

Wait up, Cagey, you've got company. At the very least, he'd try to keep his sense of humor in the afterlife.

Yup, I'm dead. Wow. Didn't even hurt. At least Dinah was safe. Vincent assumed she was probably back at the arch, waiting—

Before he finished his thought, Vincent could see again. The flash of white light had passed. More impressive, he could *feel* again (namely, his behind, which had just landed on solid earth).

He checked himself for wounds, finding only scrapes from the break-in and the fight. He hadn't been shot at all, which meant that he must have survived his first encounter—although it had left him completely exhausted.

Dinah groaned next to him. Apparently, she was undergoing similar issues with her backside. "How can all this be happening?" she asked to no one in particular.

Vincent flopped onto the ground. He had no answer—and frankly, he'd stopped wondering about the hows and whys. It *was* happening, and that was all that mattered for the moment. They were players in some kind of game; who made the game and how it came to be counted less than how the game was played—and more important, how the game was won. The game *had* to be won, or else Dinah would die.

Dinah rubbed her head and watched poor Vincent resting on the ground. He'd won this one, she knew. She'd been chased by those bizarre hounds, which had been something of an adventure, to be sure, but had nothing to do with Cagey. Heck, she'd never even *seen* the girl. *How pathetic*, she silently chided.

She gathered the torn and soiled lengths of her skirt and held them for comfort. At least the girl-ghost had been saved, whether Dinah had played an active role or not. So maybe the next time she had to see Bali-Lali, the creature would at least be civil; after all, they'd completed the first mission.

Just as she finished that thought, Bali-Lali—speak of the devil!—caught Dinah by her shawl and lifted her into the air. She pulled Dinah close, until they were nearly face-to-freakish face—so close that Dinah was able to see that the creature's fangs actually pierced her tight-lipped smile.

"One lost soul saved, so many to go," Bali-Lali said. "Remember to return each night . . . if you'd like to keep your foolish little head." With that, the creature flung Dinah to the ground, just as child would toss away an unloved doll.

However muted Bali-Lali had been when she'd surprised Dinah, she made no efforts to mask the mechanical clanks and clicks of the cables that attached her to the ceiling now. With a single, great tug, the creature returned to her secret dwelling, sealed away as the latch slammed into place.

So, that's where we've ended up, Dinah thought, *back at the Mausoleum*. Why couldn't they have been sent back home again? This way, they'd have to make the return trip through the woods, around the garbage heap, under the tangled cords, and past the dead fawn. What hour it was, she had no idea, but she feared the sun would rise by the time they'd made it home, leaving her dead tired *and* in deep trouble with Aunt Jane.

"Vincent," she started—but nothing else came to mind. She was exhausted.

He held her, wondering all the while about what the next stage of the game would bring, and whether it could be won so easily.

THE STRANGLEHOLD

*B*y the time Vincent had returned her home and boosted Dinah through her bedroom window, she'd been too tired to understand his parting whispers. Something about tomorrow . . . something about getting through this together.

Once over the window frame, her hands had touched the deep grain of her floorboards, which she regarded as quite comfortable, considering the hour. The last noise she'd heard—from the waking world, at least—was the soft squeal of Vincent's bicycle as he pedaled for home. By the fourth squeak, she'd fallen fast asleep, her cheek resting on her long dark curls.

She dreamed of Bali-Lali, the she-spider coming into her room and calling for Dinah to return to the Mausoleum. In her dream, Dinah begged the she-spider to hide because Dr. Morstan was coming. And when he arrived (in the middle of the night, as dream logic goes), Dinah found herself barricading her closet door as Bali-Lali scratched at it from within.

"What seems to be the trouble *this* time, Dinah?" Dr. Morstan asked, glancing at Aunt Jane, who had been a stuffed piglet on Dinah's bed only a moment before. Dinah hated how thoroughly Dr. Morstan could communicate without speaking;

in a single glance, the man was capable of saying, *"Your niece has finally lost it, Jane. It's time for her to go someplace . . . special."*

All the while, Dinah pressed her back against the closet door, which bent outward as though made of rubber. Within, Bali-Lali chortled and hissed.

"You can't hear her?" Dinah pleaded in her dream. "You can't see what she's doing?"

Aunt Jane covered her eyes. It was true, she seemed to think, the girl was beyond her help, maybe even dangerously psychotic.

"I'm *not* crazy!" Dinah screamed. "Ask Vincent."

"There is no Vincent," Dr. Morstan answered, as if lecturing a five-year-old. "We've been over this, Dinah. You're alone. In the end, you're always alone. And now it's time. It's time you come with me." He reached into his case, which he hadn't been carrying a moment ago, freeing a clasp. His hand emerged holding a syringe. When he squeezed the base, a spray of cloudy chemical shot across the floor before Dinah.

"No more Vincent. No more ghosts," Dr. Morstan chided.

As he drew near, Aunt Jane rose from the bed, hands set to restrain Dinah—and Bali-Lali pushed on the door until the wood cracked. Splinters drove into Dinah's spine like daggers—no, like *needles*. Where they pierced her, blood seeped from her flesh into the blushing door as icy fluid streamed into her veins. The chilling pain forced her ever closer to Dr. Morstan.

"It's for the best," he reminded her, "always for the best."

Dinah awoke, her head snapping to attention. Darkness crept into her bedroom; outside, evening reigned, and she was still on her bedroom floor. Her back ached from the awkward position into which she'd curled up to rest, and she was freezing without her bedsheets. But none of that mattered because she'd heard something . . . something loud enough to wrest her from sleep. Something real.

Her mind raced: Had those freakish dogs followed her from their world to here? *Don't move*, she commanded herself. The way her back felt right then, she was sure it would crack if she turned even an inch, and whatever had made the noise would hear her.

Outside, the moon had nearly completed its celestial arc, leaving Dinah's room in darkness. According to her bedside clock, it was three o'clock in the morning, on the nose.

A lock of hair fell in her face, tickling her cheek, but she refused to move.

And then, she heard it again: a sound like a rake through tall grass, like a scythe through chaff, outside on the St. Lyman's property.

Slow as she could, Dinah straightened herself, making sure her head remained below the window frame. Then, having heard the sounds again—there were several sources—and having figured that they were far enough away, she grabbed the window's frame and pulled herself up to peek.

There they were: the Stiltwalkers, out on the lawn. She'd seen them before, but never in the middle of the night, and never after rousing from a nightmare. How had she described them to Vincent in the past? As human skeletons, sure enough, but with occasional patches of leathery, tight skin here and there—over half the face, across a shoulder, wrapped around the neck like a fluttering scarf. Below the knees, however, their leg bones were extraordinarily long, like the false legs of a circus stiltwalker—hence the name she'd given them.

The very first time she'd seen one was the only time they'd actually terrified her: She'd been eleven then, and she'd awakened for some reason shortly after Aunt Jane had tucked her in. Something circular had cast a shadow across her room, silhouetted by moonlight and an exterior lantern. When she'd looked out the window, she'd seen one of them peeking in at her, its eyes hollow, its mouth open as if it wished to speak or cry, but lacking vocal cords to so much as whimper. She'd hidden under her sheets; by the time she'd peeked out again, it had disappeared.

Since then, she'd sometimes watched them at night, ambling back and forth across the lawn, shoulders slumped, faces aimed at the earth beneath them. She no longer feared them, or at least she feared them much less than the entities who stalked the *interior* of the house at night—the shades of hospital staff who Dinah guessed must've once worked for St. Lyman's. Actually, she pitied the Stiltwalkers at times, mostly because they couldn't speak, and because they looked terribly sad as they slogged along the property, their long bones slicing at the grass.

Maybe because of her experience at the Mausoleum that evening, Dinah had a new insight. She saw their long legs as curses; every time she'd watched them, they seemed to be searching the grounds—but should they ever find what they sought, how could they ever reach it? They walked always, and no amount of leaning would gain access to the distant earth. They would need help.

Oh God, Dinah thought as her heart began to race.

The logic pieced together all too well, whether it was ultimately true or not. She had been contracted by the Mausoleum to free trapped spirits. What had kept her sane until now was the idea that there would be a finite number of souls in need of saving—that the cemetery grounds were only so big. But what if it never ended? What if, after facing the ghosts out in the woods, she would be assigned new spirits like these Stiltwalkers? And after that, the resident hospital staff? Or the governess, who tormented her most of all?

Feeling faint, she promptly shut the curtains to hide the image of those sad souls outside, running to her bathroom.

There it was: her daily dosage of Dr. Morstan's chalk stuff.

Every single day, assuming the doctor hadn't arrived to personally provide the meds, she poured the gunk down her drain. Tonight, though . . . she touched her chest and felt her heart beating against her ribs. It might never end, she realized. This Mausoleum contract might never go away.

There are so many unhappy souls. More and more every day. You can't save them all.

She couldn't save them all.

The drug tasted exactly as she'd expected—powder poorly mixed, like cement mixing in her gut—but tonight, she needed it. She saw no other way to escape Bali-Lali and the contract. As she crept toward her bed, she could already feel the cobwebs spinning through her brain.

☾

She heard a bird outside her window. Any other day, she'd have decided that her head was still too cloudy to do anything but sleep (minus the nightmares, thank you very much). But this morning, Dinah wanted to open her eyes and see—see whether she'd been awakened by the same bird she'd freed last night. Wouldn't that be something? Wouldn't that be hopeful?

She rolled over to peer out the window. *Oops*, she thought, *we left the window unlocked last night.* It was even a crack open. Silly move . . . if Aunt Jane had crept in there as she sometimes did while Dinah pretended to be sleeping, she would have discovered the open window. A lecture would've followed. And of all the things Dinah needed right now, lectures were at the bottom of her list.

Through the glass, she saw the morning sun shining on the leaves in the trees outside. Somewhere out there was her winged, singing alarm clock. She decided not to look for the bird after all; it was far better to believe the Mausoleum bird had come to visit her, either to say "thank you for choosing my vault" or simply to watch over her for a while.

As Dinah sat up, Dr. Morstan's chalk stuff gave her head a final spin before it lost its potency altogether. For the first time, she was actually thankful for the goop; although she'd had fewer than eight hours of sleep, she felt well rested.

She folded down the covers and walked to her vanity. Time for school.

Considering that Ms. Warren, her math teacher, wouldn't be demanding that Dinah go grave-diving any time soon, heading to class sounded like a great way to avoid thinking about the night before—or even worse, about *tonight*. After all, Bali-Lali had insisted Dinah return this and every evening until the job was complete.

She began brushing out the knots in her hair, along with the occasional leaf and twig, thinking absently about the day ahead. School would be great today, certainly; it would pass the time and give her the illusion of living an ordinary life. But here was the thing: Could she maintain a façade of actually caring about what happened in classes or hallways at this point? How do you care about love triangles and football games when you know for certain that the people around you could one day end up restless ghosts?

For a moment, she feared that she might spend all day watching the other kids pass. She imagined her mind taking tallies: The bespectacled nerd in the corner . . . the heavyset girl with the splotchy cheeks . . . if they died today, outcast and humiliated as they were, might they become tormented souls, too? And would Dinah have to rescue them?

She glanced at herself in the mirror. There in her reflection, she saw *it*, the mark of the Mausoleum—the six-legged bug with the alarm-clock head, thick and black against her white flesh. The rounded bottom of the alarm clock nestled in the valley where her collarbones met, whereas the body followed her breastbone, curving slightly as if the curled tail might whip at her heart.

Suddenly, Aunt Jane was at her door. "Dinah? I have your breakfast ready."

Her words were benign enough, but Dinah knew by experience that the subtext in Aunt Jane's voice meant something was up; maybe Aunt Jane had noticed Dinah's absence after all.

"Dinah?" Aunt Jane continued. "Open the door!"

Instinctively, Dinah covered her tattooed neck and chest as best she could. "Go away! Don't come in!" How, *how* had this happened? Could the mark be removed? She turned back to the mirror again.

And the mark was gone. For all appearances, it had never touched her in the first place.

Time to get dressed, Dinah thought. Time to busy herself so she wouldn't start thinking about this too much—because if she thought too much, she'd fall into the ice ocean again . . . and one of these days, she believed she was going to drown.

At the breakfast table, Aunt Jane was reading the *Daily Eagle*, Bizenghast's local paper. She read it every morning, or at least when the little punk delivery kid decided he'd ride by and toss her the paper she'd paid for. *Kids today*, she reflected over her third cup of coffee, *they have no sense of responsibility to adults*.

She *hated* thinking things like that. It aged her, and she already felt much older than she was. That was the curse of parenthood, perhaps one of many—that you leave behind your freedom in order to build something solid, something secure, for the new generation. That was fine, and it made sense—except that Ms. Jane Addison had never chosen to have a child.

Not that she was complaining. *Oh God*, she thought to herself, *I hate feeling sorry for myself.*

She'd been up since five that morning, after having heard some shambling about last night at who-knows-what hour in the morning. She'd been tempted to rush into Dinah's room again, as she had in the past—but Dinah was getting older, and Jane wanted to give the girl something resembling trust, even if she couldn't promise her freedom. That part was up to Dr. Morstan. He was the expert on these things. Jane was merely an aunt who had inherited some property, and with it a daughter . . . one she loved enough to make hard decisions for her.

She heard the water running in Dinah's room. Soon, she'd have to fit in a lecture before school. For the moment, though, Jane counted herself lucky; the delivery boy had decided to grace her with news of the day, so it was best to enjoy it—tomorrow, she might find the paper down the street in a ditch, in a wandering dog's mouth, or not at all. Ah, small-town life in Bizenghast . . .

On that note, Jane Addison read the headline for that day's feature story: "'Second Graveyard' Theory Still Disputed."

Sheesh. This was what happened when you gathered up a few dozen golden oldies in a town where there was nothing to do but wait for Social Security checks and spin yarns.

She shook her head and rubbed her eyes. The caffeine had roused her, but it did nothing for her weary eyes as she read.

Evidently, the local newspaper felt it was newsworthy when visitors spread tales about discovering a mysterious graveyard hidden in the woods that they were never able to find again. Jane sighed, wondering if she flipped through the pages she'd find a story about Dr. Frankenstein creating a child for his monster and its bride, or an article about the local werewolves meeting for their monthly tea.

Here was an amusing waste of ink:

"'My husband and I were out hiking in the woods when we found this enormous place, right in the middle of a field,' Maryann King told the Daily Eagle. *'It was like a huge graveyard with really big towers that looked kind of like horses or something. . . .'"*

And wouldn't you know it, when this couple returned later on with other people, they couldn't find the place again. What a shock.

There was, however, some merit to the story: It led with a bit about an investigation into Bizenghast's town records, and the note that many of the death certificates issued between 1701 and 1950 had no correlation with plots in the official local graveyard. Now, that *was* interesting, because it was rooted in fact, not rumor and nonsense. That part, at least, was decent reporting, not kid stuff. Despite being filled with senior citizens, this town needed to grow up, Jane mused. Everybody had to some time.

Dinah finally entered the kitchen, where she began pouring herself a bowl of cereal.

She'd have to rush if she was going to make it to school on time, Jane realized, and Dinah had already missed enough of her classes already. It was embarrassing—what a terrible parent Jane must have seemed . . . but what could be done?

Jane rose from the table. Standing made her feel more authoritative. "Dinah," she said, "I don't know what you think you were doing last night, but you are *not* to leave this house again without permission."

Dinah didn't even look up. "I was in bed," she muttered.

"Dinah, I know you went somewhere with that boy. Now, I'm not going to tell you again. . . . It's for your own good."

With that, Aunt Jane left the room. It felt like the right moment—or at least the best moment to punctuate the scolding, given that she felt like a fraud, as usual. She'd never wanted to lecture anyone. She'd had a fun life before the accident, living in Colorado, directing lectures at no one but herself. Then, *she'd* been the young and foolish girl.

☽

That evening, Dinah left her house without permission—again. In the past, she might have done it out of boredom, or to escape the phantoms creeping through the halls—but this time, Dinah *had* to sneak out. Her life depended on it . . . literally.

She'd met with Vincent just down the street from St. Lyman's, walking with him in almost complete silence for much of the trip to the Mausoleum. During the walk, she reflected on how strange her day at school had been.

For one thing, it had moved so quickly, likely because going to school, taking notes, and bearing her teachers' remarks on her attendance records was a treat compared to her new nightly responsibility.

But the stranger thing was something she herself had done. She'd surprised herself twice between classes—twice, she'd ran into Vincent in the hallway . . . and found herself looking the other way as she passed him. Why, she couldn't say.

Why did I deliberately shun the only person who knows for certain I'm not crazy? Why did I avoid someone who saved my life last night?

The answer came to her that evening as she walked among the thinning trees which marked the opening to the field in which the Mausoleum lay: Vincent was a reminder of her contract. By night, she wanted him near, to protect her; but at school, with "normal" kids milling about and talking about clothes and concerts to be seen, she preferred to forget that ghosts existed, to forget that part of her life. Seeing Vincent made forgetting impossible.

"I don't want to go back, Vincent," she said. "Can't we just turn around and go to your house?" She knew his answer would have something to do with that wretched creature from the night before, so she added: "How would Bali-Lali know where to find me?"

"It's probably not smart to find out," he said, flatly ending the discussion. He addressed her as an expert repairman spoke to a customer who'd asked a silly question; he was brief, to the point, and condescending enough to prevent more questions on the subject.

She felt a pang, recognizing that as much as he cared for her, he'd likely chosen to take the lead here because she hadn't handled herself well thus far. But what did he expect from her? She hadn't asked for any of this graveyard lunacy. She'd just been unlucky enough to be the random dummy who touched the black key and got locked into a terrible bond.

She sighed as Vincent pulled at the Mausoleum door, through which they'd enter before selecting the next soul to save—but the door stayed stubbornly shut.

Vincent pulled harder, to no avail. "Why won't the door open? It opened last time!" he muttered.

Dinah allowed him time to think, not wanting to get in his way, and after a minute, he answered himself. "What did Bali-Lali say? 'Bring gold next time'?"

Here, Dinah knew she could be of some help. "I have a gold locket." She removed it from around her neck and handed it to him, feeling like a child passing a tool to a parent—compliant and naive.

"Worth a shot." He turned to the statue of the blindfolded and winged beggar woman who guarded the door, tossing the locket into her plate. The gold pinged off the plate wall, spun around its rim, and finally landed dead center, just as the door clicked open.

Terrific, Vincent thought to himself. *Not only are we locked into these missions, but we also have to give these creatures gold in order to do their work.* That was going to get hard someday, he realized, and he contemplated whether there was a cheaper way to go.

At present, though, he and Dinah had a job to do.

They walked the graveyard until they both stopped to read the same placard:

"Let it never be said,
I was so justly bound,
That my soul quite deserving,
Was put into the ground

In hands hard as iron,
I hold keys hard as rock.
In places of fortune,
Will you find the lock."

They stood in silence, trying to figure out the riddle. Vincent found himself wondering why every stone had a riddle in the first place. After all, didn't Bali-Lali *want* these souls saved? Maybe, though, the riddles represented the spirits' ambivalence about being redeemed. On one hand, each spirit might want help; on the other, each had been twisted enough to resist release in the first place . . . hence, the complicated riddles.

As Vincent pondered this, Dinah, perhaps thinking it too much work to solve this riddle, had become distracted. "Vincent, I think there are children buried here, too," she said.

"Never mind that."

Vincent tried to focus on this site rather than whatever tangent Dinah had gone off on this time. In the end, they'd have to solve all the riddles here, so it didn't make sense to set this grave aside unless they'd first given it their best shot.

He inspected the statue of a young man that was associated with the riddle. This was a handsome, albeit sad figure, and he held in one hand a ring of keys—keys "hard as rock," as in the riddle—leaning with the other arm against a broken Grecian column, the base of which was covered in artful carvings of . . . what kind of plants were those?

Shamrocks.

"I think I found it," Vincent declared.

"I think I found it. Look, 'places of fortune' must mean shamrocks." Sure enough, a keyhole had been hidden amongst the foliage.

With that, Dinah's focus returned to the riddle, so she leaned over to relieve the statue of its keys. She found the right one—the first she'd tried, actually—and discovered that once she turned the key, the ground opened near them, revealing a passage into this ghost's world. *Simple as that*, she thought. She hoped all the riddles they'd have to face would be as easy.

"Another doorway into another dream," she murmured, and she liked the sound of that, even though she felt the base of her spine tingling and the hairs on her neck rising.

As Dinah noted the chill in the atmosphere, they passed through the doorway into the new realm, experiencing a rush of movement and air similar to the last time they'd been transported into a spectral dream.

This time, however, they landed before a stately home nearly as large as a castle. Whether it really was a castle, Dinah couldn't tell for sure, but she was certain royalty of some kind must've lived there.

The structure was built of black stone, and rows upon rows of windows lined the first and second floors. The gables atop the residence also bore windows. But on either side of the building, the buttresses that had supported the structure of heavy, arched window designs were gone; they'd cracked and scattered, and they now lay in pieces across the estate grounds.

Upon seeing this, Dinah wondered if the landscapes of the dead were always in decay.

The most distinctive feature was that the mansion was split in two, and its halves were as jagged and unwelcoming as the bleak, craggy mountains in the distance.

Dinah and Vincent stood at the base of a length of stairs that led to the front entrance. "Great," Vincent remarked. "Another house."

Yes, Dinah thought, *another house*. Only this time, she was going to enter it along with Vincent. No more waiting outside, no matter how scared she might become. She'd learned a valuable lesson last time: Dogs with upside-down jaws were no fun at all.

"It's huge," she answered.

When they heard a voice nearby, they noticed for the first time that a man in the garb of a royal servant sat calmly on a boulder at the other side of the archway leading to the mansion.

Dinah decided he looked safe enough, considering his pleasant, calm smile and his silly hair; it looked to her as if someone were aiming an invisible blow dryer at the servant's head, making his hair flip up into a curling wave. This thought made her giggle.

"I be the footman here," the man explained. Dinah felt even more at ease with him once she heard his cockney accent. "Don't bother 'bout that 'ouse. No one lives there anymore, ever since 'is lordship done away wit' 'imself."

So, this *was* the home of someone lordly after all. The more the man told her, the more she felt she could actually try to help on this mission, much as she hated being there.

The footman chatted on in good cheer, especially good cheer considering the tone of his message. "See, 'e couldn' marry the girl what he was in love wit', so he put the both of 'em away to rest. Now 'is lordship's ghost dances the night away every evenin' in the ballroom. Don't give a mind 'bout anything anymore."

Dinah smiled at the footman and was about to thank him for his help when she noticed that Vincent had already started to run up the stairs; she refused to be separated from him, so she ran along after. Ahead, she could hear Vincent mumbling something about the footman being pretty darn convenient.

"This place is so big," she called to Vincent between breaths. "Where do we even start?"

She found her answer even as she asked the question, though—as did her partner. "I think I hear . . . music? Follow me," Vincent instructed.

A quick walk about the structure revealed that it had suffered greatly since its lordship had stopped caring for it. Dinah and Vincent found a massive breach in the wall, through which they could gain entrance (along with a Mac truck, if necessary, considering its gaping size).

75

As quietly as possible, they stepped through to the interior, following the sound of string instruments—the quivering warble of violins here, the deep, tremulous quaver of a cello there. Somewhere nearby, musicians played—and if the footman was to be believed, dancers danced, as well. And where there was dancing, there was the lord of this house.

They soon found the source of the music—closed behind ten-foot-high doors. Combining their strength, they opened one of the heavy portals, together peeking inside.

The footman had been right. Here, in a ballroom lit by a periphery of candelabras, ghostly guests danced, dressed as if for a masquerade. *How curious*, Dinah thought, *they're all spinning in pairs like figures atop a jewelry box.* The figures twirled and twirled about, mechanical and constant in their patterns. Then, as one pair of dancers spun near Dinah, she noticed a new detail: The man had an enormous windup crank embedded in his back. The same went for his lady as she passed.

Dinah's first thoughts returned to Bali-Lali and the gears that seemed to govern her movement, but these dancers were unlike that beast entirely; they were lovely and genteel, reserved and graceful. Plus, the cranks in their backs suggested innocent marching toys, unlike Bali-Lali entirely.

Vincent whispered in Dinah's ear, pointing out a young man who resembled the statue they'd discovered earlier: "Look, that must be him. What's he doing?"

"He's . . . dancing by himself."

Sure enough, the youth danced alone, yet he fixed his arms upright and in position, as if holding an absent partner.

Dinah noticed that he was the only dancer without a windup crank. On the other hand, he was also the only dancer wearing a strange sort of lock on his chest. Dinah studied it for a moment; the lock, as adorned as a crown, sat squarely against the young man's breastbone, strapped on by cords wrapping around his midsection. Surely, Vincent was right: This guy had to be the one.

"He looks pretty sad," Vincent added. "Okay, look. See that lock on his chest?" He placed his hand on the small of Dinah's back, gently directing her attention to a far wall. There, she saw nothing but keys—keys hanging by chains from the ceiling, keys leaning against furniture that contained nothing but keys . . . golden keys, silver keys, brass keys, bejeweled keys—hundreds of them waiting to be tried, not counting the keys within the shelving. "Maybe one of those keys over there fits the lock on his chest."

I hope not, Dinah thought. They'd be there all night, trying and eliminating one key after another, praying for a lucky break. In the meantime, she had an aunt at home waiting for a reason to call the doctor and have Dinah taken away—and never mind school the next morning, or getting a decent night's sleep, for that matter.

Despite these thoughts coursing through her head, Dinah had just begun to compliment herself on her ability to remain calm, all things considered, when suddenly she felt a terrible shove pushing her toward the dance floor. Vincent had pushed her!

"You distract him," he said. "You're cute. He'll notice you."

Cute? Dinah wasn't even sure how to respond to that, but she didn't have time to, anyway—the moment her foot touched the dance floor, courtesy of Vincent's shove, she noticed glimmering lights dancing around her and a strange transformation taking place. It began at her toes, where her black strappy shoes changed into bejeweled, glimmering footwear worthy of a lord's masquerade. Her heels grew higher, and the gemstones gleamed even in the candlelight. Along her legs, thighs, hips, and all the way up to her shoulders, her skirt and coat melded and lightened, becoming a sparkling dress. It was then that she felt a weight atop her head; when she reached up to touch her hair, she discovered a tiara there.

All of this—the ghosts, the split mansion, Vincent's jostling, the transformation of her clothes—it was all happening so fast. Yes, she felt obligated to pitch in this time and be a part of the solution, but exactly what had Vincent been thinking when he'd decided *she* should be given the job of distraction, all by herself among these—

"Ro . . . Rosette?" she heard the young man say.

The handsome youth with the locked heart called across the floor to her, from behind a man dressed as a pirate and his dancing partner. He'd misidentified her, but Dinah had no doubt he was speaking to her and to her alone.

"My little Rosette? Is that you?"

Before Dinah could respond (not that she had the slightest notion of what she might say), he was upon her, taking her by the arm and urging her toward the center of the floor. "Come dance with me, precious," he said, and she felt a secret willingness to dance with him despite herself. And anyhow, to solve the Mausoleum case, she would have to distract him as Vincent had instructed, so she might as well follow his lead and let the handsome spirit take her in his arms—which he did, resuming the same position he'd assumed earlier while dancing alone.

It seemed to Dinah that she fit his embrace perfectly. He held her close, the line of her dress brushing his lockbox. It was as if they had been lovers for years, and she felt her mind wandering, as if lazily dreaming while dancing with her trusted companion.

In this dreamlike state, her eyes wandered above the candles, where, framed in gold, they spotted a portrait of a young girl—a portrait that looked *exactly* like Dinah.

The girl in the portrait wore period clothes, certainly, but her black hair curled just like Dinah's, and she even had Dinah's sharp blue eyes. The girl might as well have *been* Dinah, the resemblance was so precise.

Is that . . . Rosette? Dinah wondered. *She looks . . . just like me!*

Meanwhile, Vincent sat before a horde of keys and was confronted with two major dilemmas. First, he had to guess which one would be the key to the young man's heart, as it were. If he took a guess from among all the keys here, he reckoned he had about a one in two thousand chance of getting it right, so *that* was terrific news. Second, he'd have to test each guess by actually physically inserting said key into the man's lock. Impossible—and tedious, to say the least.

To Vincent, the seemingly impossible situation with the keys resembled the riddles on the Mausoleum gravestones. He'd previously theorized that these restless ghosts had some kind of internal struggle—craving redemption and obstinately clinging to their miserable afterlives—and that reluctance explained why Dinah and he had to solve riddles before lending the spirits a hand. Vincent wondered if his current plight was analogous; and if it were, then there must be some kind of clue around here somewhere. The part of this noble that *didn't* want help found representation in the form of the three bazillion keys before Vincent . . . but what about the other part—the part that sought peace?

As Vincent was pondering this, he happened to spot a slender white mouse—wearing a poufy, feathered hat, no less—scurrying over a pile of keys. When it paused to stand upon its hind feet (as if to mock the dancers), Vincent noticed that in its mouth, the little squeaker held a golden key with a handle shaped like two adjoined diamonds.

That *had* to be the right key—two diamonds were melded together, just as this lord had intended for Rosette and himself to be. Vincent froze so as not to frighten the mouse away; he didn't want the key to disappear into a hole in the wall.

"Easy, buddy," he whispered to the mouse. "Stay right there." If that were truly the proper key, Vincent could make all this craziness vanish, and Dinah and he could return home. . . .

Unfortunately, the mouse had little interest in helping the lord of the manor, and he scampered off at top speed.

Vincent and the Mouse

The dance, Dinah had to admit, was playing out wonderfully. She knew none of the steps, but it turned out she didn't need to—the lord of the manor spun her along gracefully until she recognized the pattern and was able to follow it. With dancing, there was always a pattern one could master; once you found the rhythm, it was easy to determine what must come next by virtue of said pattern . . . unlike so many other aspects of life.

This poor boy, she thought. Why couldn't he marry Rosette? Why did he throw away his life for her? And Rosette herself . . . whatever happened . . . ?

Caught up in the pattern of the dance and the rhythm of the music, Dinah found her thoughts drifting back to her discussion with the kindly footman:

What had the footman said? He couldn't marry the girl that he was in love with, so he put both of them to rest? Or something like that. Both of them . . . So, the boy killed himself, but only after he'd—

She felt a dagger digging at her flesh.

The young man leaned close to her. "Mother says we can't marry, Rosette. But I have a plan."

"Hey! Get back here!"

"Of all the absurd situations to be in," Vincent muttered venomously. He envied Dinah's role in this mission. All she had to do was dance, and she was likely enjoying herself. In the meantime, here Vincent was chasing a white mouse in a funny hat under the feet of phantom nobles. Yippee.

He grabbed and nearly caught the little beastie, but it was slimmer than it appeared (it so happened that this mouse was particularly fluffy), and with an athletic leap, it escaped Vincent's fists. From there, it landed atop the boy's head, where it may or may not have purposely scratched Vincent's scalp with its tiny claws before scampering another five feet away.

The two opponents then squared off, staring each other down. This was it, a kind of mortal combat, except that it was between boy and mouse, so it wasn't really life threatening (at least not for the boy).

The boy glared. The mouse in the feathered cap glared.

The boy grabbed hold of a trusty cane.

The mouse nibbled on the golden key. (The key did not taste very good.)

Just then, Vincent heard his companion cry out: "Vincent, hurry with that key!" and he knew it was time to take care of business.

"This one's going over the fence," he said as he wound up before swinging the cane at the white mouse.

If there were a baseball-like game involving the striking of a hat-loving mouse with a cane, surely Vincent would find himself in the mouse-ball hall of fame, for he nailed the poor vermin straight toward Dinah, whereupon she caught the loose key (a worthy feat in itself).

"I got it!" she shouted. As Dinah inserted the key, the surrounding dancers turned to see what all the fuss was about and the young noble twisted his body to drive his dagger deep into his dancing partner's back.

Click.

The key turned. Dinah had managed to unlock the young noble's heart, and his spirit found release. As he went to reach for Dinah, he noticed his former love, Rosette, hovering above him. Now, bathed in white light, the angelic lord ascended, joining his soul mate.

"I forgive you," Rosette said, and the two floated toward the heavens, where Dinah hoped they would find peace.

Upon discovering that her dress had reverted to its original form—which was less lovely but much more comfortable—and that the guests in the ballroom all had disappeared—leaving Vincent and her alone there—Dinah stared after the soaring lovers until she could no longer see them.

"I don't understand. . . . How could he kill the girl he loved? It doesn't make any sense."

"It's love, Dinah. It doesn't always have to make sense." Vincent turned to see her eyes, but she stared forward, watching the angels until they appeared as doves against the clouds.

Fair enough, Dinah reasoned. *After all, not much else in life makes sense, anyway.*

☽

Rosette and Ironbound

Curiously, during the walk home, Dinah felt wide awake. What time it was, she had no idea. Surely, she should have been asleep for hours already, yet the weariness hadn't hit her at all.

When they reached her window, she climbed in. This part was awkward: She needed a boost from Vincent, who raised her until her belly reached the base of the frame, and then she could scoot herself the rest of the way through, finally plopping onto her bedroom floor—more or less making a fool of herself in front of her companion in the process. The good news was that she didn't have to care; it was only Vincent, after all. No need to impress.

She turned to him before closing the window. "Hey Vincent?"

"Yeah?"

He was blushing. Why was he blushing? No matter. "Thanks for helping me," she said.

"Always a pleasure."

And tonight, she thought she understood what he meant by that, to some degree. It was true that she still hated the idea of having to do Bali-Lali's dirty work, just as much as she hated being unlucky enough to get stuck with the contract in the first place. But tonight, she'd been sort of useful. At the very least, she hadn't cowered in a corner. That was *something*, and that satisfactory thought might even award her a decent night's rest.

THE COMING STORM

*A*bove Vincent, moss and ivy lay claim to the latticework he'd nailed up three months before, shortly after his parents had left on their current vacation.

On this trip, much like on their last voyage, they were traveling around the world from Who-Knows-Where to Pick-a-Spot, and they'd no doubt bring him some useless souvenir bought at Random Tourist Trap. That was exactly what Vincent needed: another magnet, or maybe a new snow globe from an ironically arid country.

Within the tangle of greenery, insects crept. And when two bees buzzed by, Vincent wondered whether they might report this location to their queen as a prospective spot to build a hive.

Vincent loved this outdoor world.

His family estate—which had been won by the efforts of his grandfather, proprietor of a hotel enterprise—was such a large property that Vincent had no trouble imagining himself completely alone when he willed it . . . which was almost always. Except for when Dinah was near; then, he was happy to have company.

This place was his and no one else's, and if his parents regarded it as an eyesore upon returning from their long trip, then that was their problem. Maybe they should've thought of the consequences of leaving their only son home for weeks, sometimes months, at a time.

The ramshackle home he'd built just off his parents' house was a work in progress, constantly developing. Recently, he'd even dragged a bathtub out there—which was where he was currently surveying the scene from, allowing the water in the tub to warm him as the breeze tingled the flesh on his bare back. He'd set soap and shampoo out here on a broken column, among the plants and the treasures he'd found throughout Bizenghast, too—but as he reached for them, he discovered a most peculiar development: On the inside of his right wrist, in thick black lines over his thin blue veins, he found the marking of the Mausoleum.

"What is this?" he said aloud, although he knew he was alone. He touched the design, running wet fingers over the clock head and spiraling tail before rubbing against the six legs—to no avail. "Well, there's no scrubbing this thing off," Vincent said, and that was the end of the matter. For him, it was simple—he now wore the mark of the Mausoleum. He didn't know why that was, but it was okay by him all the same. Anyway, he imagined that Dinah might have a marking, too, which gave them something in common.

He closed his eyes and watched the bees. Yes, he sighed, the bees certainly were going to make a new home on his family's property. Someone might as well.

Dinah knew Vincent well enough to bypass his family's house and head directly into the backyard, where she found him fiddling with repairs on the greenhouse/home/hideout he'd made in the weeks since his parents' most recent departure.

The place creaked as she entered—even a calm spring breeze could made the structure groan—but she never worried whether its filched doors or pilfered, half-nailed walls might collapse upon themselves. She trusted Vincent.

She'd arrived earlier than usual, seeing as her aunt would be working late that night. Good thing, too: Aunt Jane was becoming increasingly frustrated with Dinah's mysterious disappearances. Hopefully, an earlier beginning would lead to an earlier night, which might allow Dinah to crawl into bed before her aunt checked on her. Dinah knew that was almost too much to wish for, though. She was happy that at least Aunt Jane caught her only *some* of the time; if she found out Dinah was going out every night, then there'd really be trouble.

"You're lucky your parents are always traveling," Dinah said as she watched Vincent gather some doodads and transport them from one corner of his home to another, in a pattern only Vincent himself could grasp. "They treat you like an adult and let you live by yourself."

"Yeah, lucky," he answered.

Dinah caught something in his eyes, something that told her the subject matter angered him. She'd almost never seen him angry before.

He continued: "I wonder what they'll say when they finally come home and see my little house. Or maybe they'll just keep sending money and never come home."

Could be worse, Dinah thought. *Could be much worse*. She changed the subject.

"I don't know why you live out here in the yard. Why build all this junk into a house when you already have one?"

"It isn't junk! Just look at all this," he said, gesturing about. He presented, for instance, a headless monument of a mounted soldier (which prompted Dinah to wonder how on Earth Vincent had dragged it there, although she wasn't going to interrupt him to ask, considering his current mood), a bust of a woman made entirely from dried and hardened tangles of vine, and still another headless statue, this one holding two bowls that birds were using as bathing pools. Though she wouldn't admit it, the statues freaked her out a bit—first, because they were decapitated (she hoped he'd found them that way) and second, because she'd started to associate statues with her trips to the Mausoleum.

"Salvaged from the town," Vincent continued. "They'd let all this rot away in old houses rather than save it. But I saved it. I saved it all."

He spoke with such ardor that he'd almost startled Dinah. How could anybody be so consumed by saving things? *Where'd that quirk come from?* she wondered. She looked around at the walls made of old doors and lattices and window shades, the shelves and decorations rummaged from attics and basements across town, otherwise left to rot in abandoned buildings. Whom did they all belong to before?

Perhaps he noticed a look of concern on her face, because he began to lighten up. "I think it's worth something," he said. "Somebody cared enough to make these things once. It's part of our town."

Dinah stared into a fishpond Vincent had made out of bits of broken masonry. He was, she had to admit, something of a talented landscaper. But the idea still depressed her. "*Your* town, not mine."

"Tell that to the Mausoleum. That's one section of town I don't want any part of," he said, hefting a large vase.

Surprising even herself, Dinah turned suddenly, shouting, "Don't talk about it! It makes me sick at heart. I don't want to go back there again."

Why had she reacted like that? Perhaps it was the image of her own withered, blood-drained face that Bali-Lali had shown her. She'd dreamt of it before, and a day hadn't since passed without Dinah dwelling on that image. It was true she'd survived missions already, but she was convinced that someday she would die on one. She'd only endured this far because of Vincent; without him, she wouldn't stand a chance.

Vincent kept his cool, speaking to Dinah in a tone that reminded her of a nurse talking to a surly patient. She wasn't overly fond of it. "Think of the consequences. Besides, I'll be with you."

"But you don't *have* to go. You don't have a contract."

"Would you rather go alone?" he asked.

Was he kidding? There it was again: her dead face, ashen and bone dry, wrinkled like fruit left out in the hot sun. *I'm going to die, I'm going to die, I'm going to—*

She took a deep breath. She had to change the subject.

As it happened, Vincent found something new to talk about, changing the subject for her. Again and again, he was rescuing her. "Look at this," he said, pointing toward the top of one of the walls. "These are shutters from the old bell tower. Took me three hours to pry them off without damaging them."

Inwardly, she thanked him for the shift in conversation, though it hadn't helped all that much. "Yuck, little buggies and crawlies can get into your room." The idea made her think of millipedes wriggling through the gaps in the walls . . . and then, against her wishes, she began to dwell on her own corpse again, lying somewhere in the dirt, with Mr. Millipede coming for a visit. *Hello, Mr. Millipede . . . burrow a home inside my fleshy cheek and take a look through my eye—*

She forced herself to focus on Vincent, who'd grabbed another thingamabob, as if playing show-and-tell. "I got this candle stand from the transept of the cathedral."

"I want to feed the birds." She needed to see life. She needed to see *freedom.* She walked to the statue where the birds bathed and held up some of the seed that Vincent had collected. "Here, birdies. Birdies, here." To her delight, one actually flew down for a snack. Birds, it seemed, were very tame around Vincent. He had some kind of special connection with them. "They come back here a lot, huh?"

"Mostly in the winter and early spring."

Once the bird had enjoyed its fill, Dinah wandered the improvised home; one never knew what one would find at

Vincent's place, that was for sure—and it certainly kept her mind diverted.

While Vincent continued his work (what he was doing, she had no clue), Dinah found something interesting: a sketch of a girl with long black hair and fair skin. The girl's hair blew in the wind. Dinah couldn't be sure, but she suspected it might even be a representation of her.

"Well. . . ." she said idly to herself, not sure what to make of it.

From his place across the room, Vincent was still off in his imaginary plans for his little home. "I want to build an aviary, but it's so hard to find intact glass in the old houses. Sea storms have broken all the windows over the years. Maybe I can find some in the cathedral."

"A big stained glass window for the birds?" She looked up at him, still wondering whether the girl in the sketch was supposed to be her.

"Stained glass is set in bar tracery made of lead. Impossible to pry loose. I was thinking of the Lady Chapel windows." Suddenly, he smiled. "That reminds me! I have a present for you."

Dinah put down the drawing, as easily distracted by the thought of presents as a small child.

"A present? What? What?"

"Come see!"

She followed him as he walked along a crude walkway he'd built above the first floor. She considered climbing the haphazard staircase to walk with him, but . . . well, she trusted Vincent—but his architectural skills, only so much.

He called to her from above. "Something for you to make dresses from. I found pink damask in a trunk up in the town hall attic. It's still good." With that, he grabbed a rope tethered to a lever, and the folded fabric came fluttering down.

Dinah grabbed it, looking it over. *Boys*, she thought as she inspected the dated fabric; the lines of printed flowers reminded her of dining room wallpaper from an era long past. *Where do they get their sense of taste?* "Oh, it's so . . . beautiful," she said. But it was the thought that counted, after all. At the very least, the fabric was clean and fresh.

Its scent reminded her of the detergent scent of her school uniform when she'd first received it. Boys in vests, girls in skirts and sweaters . . . she thought of her classmates. She saw them so infrequently these days.

"What do they say about me at school?" she asked.

Vincent was using the rope and lever to descend to the ground floor.

"Nothing much. I told them you were on vacation."

He was protecting her again. She could tell. "Oh," she wrapped herself in the fabric like a shawl, "is that all?"

"We've got bigger things to worry about than school," he said.

Dinah knew he was right. "I don't want to go back tonight. I don't ever want to go back. But I'm afraid of what will happen if I don't. I'm afraid she'll come and find me if I don't."

Vincent came toward Dinah—who had now swathed herself completely in his gift, save for her face—pushing back the fabric that covered her hair.

"We'll keep going," he said, "until all the vaults are empty. And then, we'll forget all about it."

"Forever?" she asked, feeling like a child.

"If you like," Vincent replied.

He sunk down next to her, staring into the distance. The sun would be setting soon. From where they sat, they would have a good view of the pink-orange sky above Bizenghast's woods. Little time remained before they would make their next journey to the Mausoleum.

"Let's watch the birds." He put his arm around her, and she said nothing.

🌙

"I found the ugliest spider in my house yesterday," she told Vincent as they walked together through the forest, already in the midst of a new mission. Yesterday, while she'd been drawing a monstrous scene (lately, she found all she could draw were monsters and people trying to fight monsters), a spider had skulked out from behind her desk, crawling right over her drawing. The troubling part was that this particular spider had a human face—spider legs, spider body, human face . . . even a human head of hair.

"What'd you do?" Vincent asked.

She remembered the little bugger's face. She'd been scared at first, but the spider's expression was more of curiosity than anything else. It seemed only to want to know what she was doing, but Dinah had no love for arachnids. So, she'd trapped it under an upturned glass and gone back to her drawing. After an hour or so, it had stopped stretching its limbs in search of escape, and its expression of fear and panic had turned to resignation. Twenty minutes later, it had suffocated.

"I don't know how they keep getting in the house," she said.

"Well, it's summertime. Don't let a couple of spiders bother you. They don't hurt anything."

She hadn't told him about the fact that it had a human head, and she didn't plan to. She'd become accustomed to leaving out parts of her stories when talking to people, for fear of freaking them out. Why stop now?

"Well," she said, "they do eat other bugs, so . . . What are we supposed to be looking for this time?"

She recalled the riddle that had opened the way into this forest:

We were many long ago,
And considered such a blessing.
We were taken from our homes
Into waters black—
Distressing.
You can find us in the graveyard,
Under canopies so white.
We will show you where to wander,
If you lend a little light.

In the graveyard, they'd discovered a stone canopy ("so white," in fact), and Vincent had lit a candle under it to solve the riddle. That had led the companions into the woods where they now walked.

If someone had blindfolded her, still Dinah would've known that these were not the Bizenghast woods of today. For one, there was absolutely no junk lying around to trip over. And she didn't mean just the massive junk piles that had prompted their discovery of the Mausoleum—there wasn't even the occasional broken glass bottle or crushed cigarette box left over from some careless passerby. These woods were pristine, and fresh air wafted through the green, vibrant leaves. The place was almost peaceful, if it hadn't been for the knowledge that these woods existed to house a ghost of some kind. Knowing that, Dinah kept her guard up.

Through the silhouettes of shaded trees, Dinah sensed movement. There, she found two girls, children, walking through the illusory woods. Much as she tried to perceive them as malevolent spirits, their looks—yellow bangs and braids layered over fair, pink flesh—made it impossible to think them anything but harmless. They were kids playing in the woods, simple as that.

Dinah showed Vincent, and they ran together to approach the girls.

Dinah spoke first. "Hello there. Where are you going?"

The older of the two, who was perhaps seven or eight, spoke. "To Maggie Murdoch's. You can come with us if you like."

Dinah looked to Vincent, who shrugged. Of course they should go along, he communicated to her without saying a word. How else would they get to the heart of the mission?

They followed the girls along a path by a stream, next turning toward and climbing down a steep edge that led to the stream itself. All the while, the older of the two girls chatted. "Maggie Murdoch lived in the woods before they flooded last summer. Mother says we mustn't go there because she's a witch."

So, maybe that was how Maggie Murdoch became a ghost, Dinah surmised: She drowned in the flood. "Shouldn't you listen to your mother?"

Across the thin part of the stream, the group found good footing on a path leading toward a clearing.

"But we know better," the little girl argued. "Maggie Murdoch is a fairy woman and she knows most everything. She fixed a cut on my leg once."

At that, the younger of the girls shouted, "Maggie!"

At first, Dinah thought the girl meant only to echo her sister's love for this Murdoch woman with her shout; but as she watched the little girl run along the path, she spotted a most curious woman standing up ahead, tending something in the babbling stream.

So strange was this woman that Dinah wanted to follow the girls and meet Maggie Murdoch herself—but Vincent took her arm. "Hang back a bit. I want to see this Maggie Murdoch."

The woman, a sylvan, platinum-haired beauty, appeared outfitted only in treasures of the woods themselves. Her dress was fashioned of sewn leaves from every season, and sometimes of spun cobweb, whereas her hair fell long and shimmering beneath an odd hat consisting of deer antlers, twigs, and squirrel's fur. Behind her, the curling path ended in a simple

Maggie Murdoch

straw-roofed home, reminiscent of a house one of the three little pigs would've built.

"She seems normal enough," Vincent said after watching the woman halt her chores by the stream and meet with the children. "Except for that hilarious hat."

But what was in the stream, Dinah wondered. What had Maggie Murdoch been attending to? She leaned forward to peek, and found her answer—there were children in the water, a half dozen or so . . . all drowned, all being—what, pickled in the water? Some floated spines up, others face up, with shoulders bobbing at the surface. Their eyes rolled toward the tops of the trees above, and their bloated cheeks broke the surface of the water as if they were tiny gray islands. Dinah let out a scream.

"Dinah, what's wrong?"

"Oh my God. . . . They're all dead . . . in the water. . . ."

Vincent looked: He viewed only fresh, clean pools of water, as far as he could see. "Dinah, there's nothing there! Nothing's in the wa—"

Dinah listened for the rest of his assertion—here she was again, telling someone what she saw only to learn that the other person saw nothing. To her, it was more evidence that she should stop telling people when she saw things.

But Vincent never finished his thought. Instead, he shouted, "They're gone! Where are the children? Where'd they go?"

The companions searched the area, scanning the nearby woods. Nothing. "I don't like this," Vincent said. "Let's go. They must've gone into the house."

Together, they ran toward the Murdoch home, which lay in the center of the clearing. The door was unlocked, so they dashed inside, hoping to rescue the girls immediately—but they found no one.

This wasn't exactly a time for levity, but Dinah couldn't help but think that this place, with all its nature-infused furnishings and scattered tools, was probably the only house messier than Vincent's. "God, what a thieves' kitchen," she said.

They rummaged around, finding only basic supplies and a table with tattered cloth. Upon the cloth, without a plate of any kind beneath, Murdoch had laid out a carved, bloodied carcass of some kind, maybe from her most recent meal. Gross as it was, at least the carcass wasn't one of the girls.

"Yeah, but no children. I don't understand. . . ."

Just then, Dinah heard peals of joyful laughter outside. She turned in time to see the elder girl chasing the younger as they ran past a window. "Vincent!" Dinah called as she unlatched the frames and opened the window. Surely, she could get their attention now.

But the children were gone again.

Dinah felt puzzled. *This is crazy. Here one instant, gone the next.* How could Bali-Lali expect Dinah to help these kids if they wouldn't even remain visible!

She was about to tell Vincent they should give up and return to their gate from the Mausoleum, the broken-down chapel on the hill, but Vincent spoke first: "I think I know what's going on here. That Murdoch is a witch. And only children are affected by her spells. We're not children, so we can't see what they see."

That was all well and good, Dinah thought, but what *help* was it? Forget it. Time to call it a night as far as she was concerned. Unless . . . "I have an idea," she shouted. "Come on! Hurry!"

"Hurry? Hurry where?"

She ran toward the gate through which they'd arrived. Every dream had one, it seemed—an archway for the first adventure, a wrecked chapel here. Once he saw where she was leading, he called out between huffs, "That's the old chapel door we came through to get here!"

This probably felt like a colossal waste of time to him. "I know!" she answered. "We're going back to the Mausoleum!" She reached the door and grabbed its handle. It had opened much more easily the first time they'd been here. "We'll just go back and ask for hel—"

She opened the door . . . and entered into the interior of the creaking chapel, empty and obsolete as it was.

Moss-covered pews stood in columns and rows, and the floor appeared to be giving way under their weight. Some day soon, the pews would collapse through to the earth below.

Dinah had never tried to re-enter a gate before; thus far, after solving a mission, they'd simply returned to their world in a flash of light while the ghostly realm dissolved, being no longer necessary.

"Why is it gone?" Dinah screamed. Vincent watched behind her, perhaps hoping she'd vent her frustrations so they could return to the dream's center and try to rescue some kids. "We're no use against magic!"

For the first time, she was actually angry about her contract—her *stupid* contract. If she was going to have to work in the middle of the night for them, the least they could do was provide help when necessary, for crying out loud. "This is all your fault! Bali-Lali, we need your help!"

Vincent closed his eyes as if he were sure she was asking for serious trouble.

Dinah waited for a response but received none. That only aggravated her further: "It's your stupid contract! You're the one who wants all this done! So *do* something already! Please help us!" She heard nothing but crickets and a few birds flapping away, frightened by her tirade. She sighed, and it seemed to her that sighing and screaming were about as much as she was good for. "Come on," she said, defeated. "Let's go."

As she walked out of the chapel, things seemed . . . strange . . . different even. For instance, the chapel's door handle was set higher than she'd remembered. Also, each step she took resulted in less distance covered. And then, there was Vincent, who—

Vincent was a child. His outfit had changed to the simple effects of a peasant boy's tunic and pants.

Noticing this prompted Dinah to take a look at her own self. Her adult figure was gone, and she'd shrunk back to her childhood frame. What's more, her dress had shifted into a frock.

"Wha . . . what the . . . ?"

"Dinah, you did it! We're children!" Vincent seemed to adjust faster than her, because he was already preparing for the return trip to Murdoch's. "C'mon. We have to hurry!"

So, Dinah thought, *maybe I have the ear of the Mausoleum after all.*

Their feet now bare and covered by youthful, fair, and vulnerable skin, running over the roots and weeds smarted as they headed back through the woods to the house; they hoped to make it in time to help the children.

Even as they ran, Dinah and Vincent could see Maggie in the distance; now, as children, they were affected by Maggie's enchantments, and their younger minds could perceive her through her illusions. The witch sat with the older of the two girls on a dock by the waters. Where the youngest child had gone, Dinah had no idea . . . but now was no time to dwell, nor to search the stream for another floating body.

Dinah could hear Maggie and the girl chatting back and forth:

"You know what I saw in the woods today, Maggie?"

The two sat side by side, like mother and child. "What's that, precious?"

"I saw a beautiful lady and her husband."

Dinah cursed her child's feet; as an adult, she would've made it to the house already. But she was making progress, slow as it was, and now she could see that the girl had fashioned a human figure from sticks as she talked with Murdoch.

Now, Maggie spoke up. Her voice bubbled like the water; even from a distance, Dinah felt its lulling, lyrical power. "Well, do you know what *I* saw today, precious? I saw a lovely waterfall down in a grotto, full of the prettiest kinds of mermaids you can imagine. They were singing so gently, and combing out their shining hair with combs made from dainty shells."

Yes, Dinah found herself musing, how lovely those combs must have been. How beautiful it would be to see mermaids. . . . She unconsciously slowed, and she thought she saw Maggie Murdoch twist her pole-thin neck to smile at her for just a moment. Dinah could help this little girl, but . . . did the girl really need help? They were merely sharing a pretty tale of mermaids, and Dinah so wanted to listen. . . .

She turned to talk to Vincent. Maybe they were wrong about Maggie Murdoch; maybe she was a *good* witch, if such things existed, and all those bodies in the water were merely kids playing games. How silly!

But as Dinah turned toward him, she saw that Vincent had already bypassed the witch and the water, running straight for the house, too quickly to notice anything else around him. She guessed he didn't care much about seeing mermaids.

What a dumb boy, Dinah thought. Again, she ran toward Maggie and the girl—but now, it was partly because she wanted to know about the lovely grotto. Running as silently as she could, she listened to Maggie:

"Over and over," Maggie sang—or spoke, Dinah couldn't tell the difference, "they combed their hair until it shone like glass, or the prettiest pink pearl. Over and over and over and over and over and over . . ."

At that point, Dinah saw that Maggie was giving the girl her very own necklace!

Or . . . was it something else entirely? While the little girl dreamed of mermaids with shining hair, Maggie reached her hands over the girl's shoulders, a thin string dangling between her fingers. She sang "over and over," which made Dinah feel dreamy, and then—and this awoke Dinah immediately—Maggie twisted the string around the girl's neck and pulled. She was strangling her to death!

There was no time left, Dinah knew. She'd asked for help, and the Mausoleum had granted it: She'd been transformed into a child, so she could see Maggie Murdoch and the children, but she'd also become prone to the witch's power.

Just as Dinah was about to scream, hoping to rouse the hapless girl, Vincent came up from behind. He'd grabbed a shovel from the pile of scattered tools in the house, and used it now to smash Maggie Murdoch in the face.

"Gotcha, witch," he said under his breath.

Maggie's spell had ended. (A blow to the face with a shovel will do that to a witch.) She slumped over and dropped into the stew, as it were, her body quickly sinking into the murky water.

Dinah ran to the edge of the water, where she watched Maggie melt into the black.

As she had come to expect, Dinah watched the drowned victims spring to life, now as winged, blissful representations of themselves. The waters swirled as the freed spirits bubbled to the top and dashed across the surface of the stream into the air, giggling as they flew. Even the elder girl, who'd survived the attack, grew wings and joined her sister among the others—but not before giving her hero, Vincent, a smooch on the cheek.

Dinah watched them fly toward the heavens as the released spirits always did, but her mind reeled with ideas. First, she'd asked for help from the Mausoleum and had received it. What did that mean? Could it be that there might be a give-and-take between them? Could she expect help in the future?

But she also wondered about her parents. How could she not? Her body hadn't yet returned to young adult form, so she was about the same age as when they'd passed on that night in Drury, Pennsylvania. Watching the angels fly away begged the question: Were her mom and dad okay?

As Dinah was still just a child, though, her youthful mind wandered away from deep thoughts as quickly as they came.

Dinah turned back to Vincent, who was still red-cheeked from getting kissed, and she did something she hadn't done in a long time: She giggled.

*D*inah had stuffed her backpack for school earlier that morning—at 4:45 to be exact, according to her bedroom clock. For that matter, she'd showered, groomed, and donned her uniform all within a half hour after that. The thing was that she *had* to get to school today—especially after reading that letter from Dr. Morstan.

Sometime in the middle of the night, Dinah had left her bed to get water from the kitchen—something she wouldn't normally do, because one never knew what might reach for her in the halls at three in the morning. But the house had been quiet enough. Besides, Dinah's adventures had left her feeling slightly braver than before.

Slightly.

When Dinah had turned on the kitchen light, she'd found a torn envelope on the counter by an ashtray stuffed with cigarette butts. (Evidently, Aunt Jane had been smoking again, a habit she turned to in times of stress.) The envelope bore Dr. Morstan's return address, so Dinah read it:

Dear Ms. Jane Audrey:
After much deliberation, I contacted Dr. Weller at the Row Sanitarium in Watertown to schedule an evaluation for Dinah on the

twenty-sixth. I regret that the situation is such that I feel she would do better with twenty-four-hour professional help, in an environment most conducive to mental healing. She cannot be allowed to remain at home by herself for most of the day.

The cost of admitting Dinah to the sanitarium on a full-time basis is rather steep, but we can arrange for most of the expenses to be absorbed by your insurance. I will schedule a separate appointment for you and I to meet with Dr. Weller and go over the necessary paperwork.

Regards,

R. Morstan, M.D.

How cold that note had felt in her hands—how sterile the words, how apathetic the tone. "Regards," Dinah whispered to herself as her heart began racing and images of bindings, straps, and white walls came flooding at her. . . .

A man authorizes a terrible destiny for a young woman, and he has the nerve to sign with "regards." Better to have signed, "to hell with her."

She hadn't slept the rest of the night, but had finally nodded off out of sheer exhaustion by sunrise. Now, late for school, she rushed down the hall into the kitchen once more, adjusting her bow and smoothing her sweater and the pleats of her skirt; she looked the image of a perfectly sane student.

Aunt Jane was reading that morning's newspaper at the kitchen table. She had the letter beside her, mostly hidden behind the paper. By the smell of things, Aunt Jane had been puffing away on her cigarettes since dawn—a sure sign of stress.

Noting all this, Dinah tried to pass through the kitchen as quickly as she could, so as to leave the old home behind and make it to one more day of classes.

"Why are you out of bed?" Aunt Jane asked, her eyes still on the paper.

"I want to go to school."

Aunt Jane never glanced up at her. She *knew* what Dr. Morstan wanted to do to Dinah, and yet she couldn't even look her niece in the eyes? "You can't," she said. "Get back in bed. It's noon. School's almost over. Go to bed."

That was the end of the discussion. Aunt Jane took a drag off her cigarette and ruffled the paper. Not once had she looked at her niece.

Fine, Dinah thought as she walked the hallway back to her bedroom. *Maybe I should go to Vincent's instead. . . . Better than lying in bed all day here, and besides—*

A voice, interrupted from behind Dinah, where no one had been a moment before; it was cold and scratched, as though the speaker had choked to death on gravel.

"Playing hooky today, are we?"

Dinah turned and saw her—the governess, the one ghost who appeared more often than any other in the house. The governess wore a high-collared blouse, tightly buttoned to the neck. Her hair was kept tightly in its bun, the spectral, wrinkled flesh at her temples pulled to the point where it seemed it might tear any moment. The governess stood most often in shadow, as though she were an extension of it, and she always—always—expressed annoyance, likely resulting from the bad behavior of her long-dead St. Lyman's boys.

The Governess

Her vicelike grip froze Dinah's wrist. There was no escaping this ghost, whose hard heels were most often heard clattering along the second floor at night. Dinah had been caught before; this was the house ghost she most feared, for the episodes were long and painful.

"Inside," the ghost demanded. She pulled Dinah toward the study, where Aunt Jane kept her computer desk.

"No . . . please!"

Dinah turned to see the room, but all of its effects were gone—no computer, no designer desk, no printer and networking cables. Nothing remained. Instead, she saw rows of tightly packed grammar school desks. At each desk sat a gray-faced boy.

One boy stared at her through his only eyeball remaining in its socket.

Another might have been smiling eagerly at the sight of Dinah—but having lost his lips, now he merely clenched mossy teeth.

She could not resist the governess. When she'd tried in the past, she'd discovered that the governess' painful grip was nothing compared to having one's knuckles smashed by the edge of a ruler.

Dinah looked back once more, at the modern-day hallway, at the electric lights, at the noontime sunlight pouring through the kitchen windows. Then, the governess slammed the door, shutting out all hope and pointing to a desk in the center of the Lyman's boys. Dinah walked to it, weeping, as the putrid students breathed their sour breath, moaning in delight at the new student.

Dinah fainted when the boy adjacent to her coughed plump, squirming maggots onto her desk. Her last thought as she drifted into the black ice ocean was that Aunt Jane would probably assume she'd slammed the door in anger.

A bad temper . . . just one more reason for Aunt Jane to get rid of that crazy kid.

Mr. Wickershire wasn't one of those crazy teachers. He never lost his cool. He hadn't yelled all year, and not once had he flicked the lights on and off or slammed the door like some teachers do for attention.

Vincent enjoyed his English class most days. Actually, Wickershire was among Vincent's favorite teachers, possibly because he once talked about how Bizenghast inspired him as a writer. Whether Mr. Wickershire actually *wrote* anything, Vincent didn't know, but at least the man had something nice to say about Bizenghast. Most of his teachers, who lived in surrounding areas like Watertown and such, weren't nearly as kind.

Vincent tried his best to listen to Mr. Wickershire's lesson, which was a review session before exams:

"So, we see that ultimately, so many of the modern mythologies with which we are familiar follow similar patterns. . . .Once the Hero accepts his or her role in the universe, the Guide character—the one who advises or protects until the Hero is ready—is no longer necessary. At that point, the Guide disappears, often perishing, though he or she may return later on."

The idea was interesting, but Vincent simply had too much on his mind to focus. First of all, Dinah had missed school again, even though she'd *promised* she'd show up, which meant that she was losing out on her last opportunity to cram in information about everything her teachers had been discussing these past few weeks. That in turn meant she was likely going to fail, and the idea upset Vincent as much as if it was him who were about to flunk out. He wanted to help her any way he could, and he was frustrated that there was no way to do so.

On top of that, he'd received a telegram from his parents (and where the heck were they now that they had to send a *telegram* of all things?). As Mr. Wickershire expounded on all the Guide characters who had kicked the bucket throughout famous films and books, Vincent tugged the telegram out from beneath his binder and read it as surreptitiously as possible.

To: V. Monroe
From: V. Monroe Sr.
We're extending our travel plans for a few more months STOP Be sure to water your mother's plants and have the gardener put the perennials in STOP Wiring money for expenses to your account tomorrow STOP Keep the house clean and don't make too much work for the housekeeper STOP Love Mom and Dad

He'd read the letter three times already since its delivery that morning. It was a simple message, and he wasn't sure what he was looking for in the subsequent reads . . . maybe something like, "We miss you STOP." That would be better, because writing "love" at the bottom of a letter—or telegram—carried as much weight as "sincerely," or "regards," or "yours."

What if they learned about his adventures with Dinah? Would they worry? Would Mom and Dad, in all their "love," come flying, driving, or hoofing it home to tell him, "Stop, son! You could get yourself killed helping that crazy girl!" Would they realize they should've come home long ago?

Mr. Wickershire took questions, most of which were along the lines of, "Will this be on the test?" One boy toward the front started asking about some science fiction movie Vincent had never seen. He was about to cross his arms and nod off (nightly adventure and battles against ghosts can make you sleepy—no offense, Mr. Wickershire) when he felt a tapping on his shoulder.

The boy behind him, a bespectacled, freckle-faced kid, handed him a note. This was somewhat awkward for Vincent— until the kid pointed behind him. There, four rows back and one column over, sat a girl whose blonde hair came running down her shoulders, shining in the sunlight as she leaned on her elbow, rosy-cheeked and purposefully looking out the window.

Vincent knew her because they had mutual friends, but she'd also been his partner in a class assignment at the time when rumors were swirling about Bizenghast's great revival. At the time, she'd mentioned to him that her parents were considering investing in Bizenghast real estate, and that she thought it would be cool to be his neighbor. But in the end, it never happened, and he never got to know her better. Fate had willed it otherwise.

He read the note:

Hi, Vincent!

How are you?

Listen, some friends are going to the movies tonight, and we wanted to know if you would come, too! There's a new Hackett and Costello movie out right now. I think they save Christmas in it or something. Oh, and Dave and Dustin are going, and you know them, so . . . Anyway, I guarantee it'll be a better movie than the lame ones Wickershire always rants about! Just nod or something if you want to go, okay? It'll be fun. Promise!

Love,

Deeg

Vincent nearly laughed out loud, though he stifled it to keep from getting in trouble. Deidre—or "Deeg" as her friends often called her—had written "love" on her letter, even though they hardly knew each other. The funny part was that her "love" felt just as authentic as the typewritten version on his parents' telegram. Sure, he could believe she loved him as much as his parents did. Why not? It wasn't hard to do, and at least Deidre actually *saw* him from time to time. By that logic, he "loved" most of the people in this classroom. Hell, he even "loved" Mr. Wickershire. No reason to exclude his favorite English teacher, so long as people were tossing "love" around like it was on sale.

I love you, Mr. Wickershire.

Vincent laughed out loud, and Mr. Wickershire heard him. "Amusing stuff, Mr. Monroe?"

"Sorry, sir." Vincent paused, intending to say no more—but as Mr. Wickershire stared, he couldn't help himself: "I love you, and I love your class. Love, love, love." Some students chuckled behind him, but Vincent ignored them. They didn't get the joke.

"Not sure I appreciate the sarcasm, young man," his favorite English teacher answered, and suddenly Vincent felt bad. Maybe some things in life—things like love, for instance—were jokes, but that didn't give him the right to be a jerk.

"Actually, Mr. Wickershire," Vincent began. "I was wondering . . ."—he tried to summon a question that would convince his teacher that he really had been paying attention—"I was wondering if there are Guides who don't die, exceptions to the rule."

Mr. Wickershire's expression warmed immediately. "Well, of course. Literature is an art, not a science, so I'm sure there are exceptions to be found. However, I will say that death or disappearance is the general rule. After all, why keep a character around who's lost his or her purpose?"

With that, Mr. Wickershire turned his attention to a new subject for review, that being categories of conflict.

Vincent looked out the window, peeking at Deidre out the corner of his eye. She was pretty, and she hung out with a fun group. If he were to go out with them tonight, he was sure to have a good time.

Deidre and the rest of her crew were cool, and Vincent certainly wasn't bound to go to the Mausoleum every night, except by his own promises to Dinah. But . . . to him, those promises were as binding as a contract, as fixed as an inky stain over his blue veins. He would never, *ever* let Dinah down. She needed him, and he would always be there for her. That was all there was to it.

He turned and looked into the girl's eyes. Smiling politely, he shook his head. Vincent had other plans tonight.

THE WEEPING JESTER

*E*very night, the trip to the Mausoleum seemed to grow shorter to Dinah. She'd never timed the process (her mind being too preoccupied with survival and that sort of thing), but she felt certain that somewhere along the trails, they must've happened upon a shortcut—or that the Mausoleum itself had crept nearer. Silly, she knew, but that was her impression. Or maybe the trip just *felt* shorter, in the way that the days pass more quickly when a giant term paper or a root canal looms.

Vincent had dropped a gold earring into the Mausoleum bowl, one of a pair that his mother had left behind. She hadn't left much else, so Vincent had decided that Bali-Lali, greedy critter that she was, would simply have to deal with getting half the pair tonight, and the other on the next visit. Their supply of gold was low already, so they needed to ration.

Vincent walked under a tree with branches large and full enough to shade him from the dim moonlight.

"What's the Pythagorean theorem, Dinah?" he asked. He'd been reading from his backpack full of schoolbooks and class notes. Now they were at Math. Before that had been History.

For her part, Dinah was entirely bored. "You know we're about to enter another dream, right?"

"Sure I do. Tough to forget," he said. "But before we get to the statue, what's the theorem?"

His tutoring had made her sleepy all the way there. (Maybe *that* was why the trip felt so short—could be that she'd fallen asleep for part of it.) "Vincent, in less than five minutes our lives are going be in danger—*again*. We need to focus."

"That's true."

"Then, maybe you can stop quizzing me?"

"You'll be fine, Dinah. I'll protect you. But exam week's coming up, and you've missed too many classes."

She sighed. "I'll worry about that in the daylight."

As her friend-turned-tutor read a passage from *The Joy of Mathematics*, Dinah found herself walking absentmindedly toward a curious statue. There was nothing fearsome about this one, nor would it had stood out if the figure—a tall, skinny, wild-haired man in a waistcoat—hadn't seemed to be covering his face for some unknown reason.

Vincent's voice grew soft in the distance as he droned on about AĐ and BĐ while Dinah lifted her skirt to her ankles and ran toward the carved statue. *How curious*, she thought as she inspected him. He wasn't covering his face as he was shielding himself from—what was that granite sphere mashed against his face?

This man was shielding himself from what looked like a rotten tomato.

Well, Dinah thought, *this is as good a place as any for tonight*, so she read the marker there:

Here lies myself,
Which is unfortunate.
How about giving me a hand?

Dinah searched the other sides of the statue's marker and base for more inscribed words. There were none.

"That's it?" she asked. "No more?" Whenever she and Vincent had come to graves in the past, they'd found many long clues—whole poems, in fact, which hinted at entryways into the ghosts' dreams. What could they possibly do with three rotten lines? They didn't even rhyme! (Dinah much preferred the rhyming poems.)

Twenty yards or so back, Vincent had moved onto sine and cosine. Dinah paid him no mind. It wasn't that she couldn't have learned the math, but there was no way she could retain all those useless facts in one night—especially with the Mausoleum's distractions. Vincent was sweet for trying to teach her, but it would all come to naught in the end. She'd missed her classes, and now she'd have to accept whatever grades she earned.

She shook her head as if to redirect her thoughts toward the matter at hand. *Hand. How about giving me a hand?*

She scrutinized the poor fellow, whose faced was eternally splotched with the guts of a stone tomato. "I'll give you a hand," she whispered, and she climbed the tall, skinny statue until she reached the battered fruit. There, struggling with all her might against corrosion and age, she managed to push the fruit away from his face.

She'd expected a gateway might open for her efforts—instead, moving the tomato revealed a hidden, telescoping shaft, which was attached at the man's cheekbone. As she pulled the stone away from the statue's face, she exposed more and more of the shaft, eventually loosening a wrapped scroll, which dangled before her in the cool midnight breeze.

In the light of the moon, she read the scroll aloud:

"There once was a boist'rous crook,
Who was harder to snare than a rook.
One day to do harm,
He sneaked to a farm,
And here are the things that he took:
A moo from a cow, a puppy's bow-wow,
And even the cat's meow.
The cow couldn't catch 'im,
The dog tried to fetch 'im,
But the cat merely grinned by the plow.

The story goes, as everyone knows,
The thief ne'er bragged of the raid.
From that day forward, not a word untoward,
Nor rowdy taunts e'er made.
Yet it weren't his lung kept his crowing unsung . . .

'Twas that the—"

And here, the scroll had been torn away, leaving the poem unfinished.

"Weirder and weirder," Dinah said. "I'm not sure I'll ever get used to this place."

"There's a bright side, though," Vincent called from below. He'd arrived beside her while she'd been reading. Mercifully, Vincent had closed *The Joy of Mathematics* and sealed it in his backpack.

Dinah quickly adjusted her skirt and made a proper seat of the statue's arm before addressing him below. "What would that be?" she asked.

"Could be that the worst we'll suffer in *this* dream is bad poetry. Not the worst way to go. And don't worry, I won't ask you about rhyme scheme."

"Forget rhyme scheme, Vincent. I have this one." She cleared her throat, as if to address an audience that wasn't there.

"Yet it weren't his lung kept his crowing unsung . . ."

She grinned.

"'Twas that the cat got away with his tongue."

Suddenly, the statue of the emaciated man shifted backward, with Dinah still seated on top. She grabbed onto his knobby shoulders, hanging on for dear life until the unseen, buried gears had brought the statue to rest five feet from its starting position.

"Nice job!" Vincent said.

"Thanks. I've always felt a connection to cats. Maybe that helped." She looked below her and saw that the entryway had no stairs or ladder; rather, it was merely a rough hollow dug into the earth by hands—or even paws.

"Oh, gross. I'm not going down there! It's filthy."

"We have to. It's the way into the dream. Besides—"

"I know. You'll protect me. But this is nasty. And cramped. And what if it just stops, and we can't get back up, and we're stuck inside a hole that looks like it's been dug by a giant rabb—"

"I think we have to trust the Mausoleum a bit. We're working for them, or it, or whatever—and we're no use stuck and suffocating, so it's safe to assume this passage leads somewhere, just like the others, right?"

Dinah relented, demanding only that Vincent go first, partly because she was scared, but also because she kept wearing skirts and dresses on these adventures, and she really needed to remember to stop doing that.

Down they went, and Dinah rejoiced to find that the void opened ten feet or so down; the trouble was, it opened on *every* side, and where the ground should've been, there was a drop off into utter darkness.

Dinah and Vincent fell into the void, shouting most of the way.

At some point, Dinah realized she could no longer hear Vincent's voice. She plummeted, her skirt fluttering in the wind, for what may have been a full minute more before she landed on something fluffy and soft.

Thump.

The darkness was so complete that she could see nothing, not even her own hand as she waved it before her nose.

"Vincent?" she whispered.

No response.

"Vincent? You there?"

She feared he'd fallen onto something less fluffy and soft, something like stone—or those jagged spikes that came up from the ground in caves. (If she'd been allowed to attend her geology class the Thursday previous, she would've learned that those were called stalagmites.)

She ran her fingers across the padding beneath her, discovering that it felt like a pile of clothing—not at all the kinds of articles one might expect at the bottom of a cave. Tumbling off the pile, Dinah braced herself against the ground, where her fingers brushed against the grooves, grain, and hammer prints of wooden floorboards.

This wasn't a cave at all. Wherever she was, she was inside a building.

Once more she called out: "Vincent!"

From the black, a boney hand stretched and touched her lips. The flesh was warm, to her partial relief; at least the interloper wasn't an actual skeleton! Even so, the stranger's fingers were so lengthened and thin that each finger felt like a spider's leg prickling her flesh.

"Quiet, my dear," the stranger said, his sharp voice quaking in anticipation. "The performance is about to begin."

"Who are—?"

"Hush and whisper! Little stagehands know better!"

Nearby, unseen hands lit candles, and Dinah could see that she sat on the left side of a theatrical stage, in the wings.

Other "stagehands," as the man called them, dashed between roughly painted two-dimensional props and dusty red curtains so quickly that she couldn't discern their appearance, nor whether Vincent was among them.

Elsewhere in the dark house, beneath a chandelier missing its crystals and a ceiling painted with scenes of cracked angels, a crowd murmured, their words incomprehensible but hurried.

Dinah absently touched her leg and noticed that she no longer wore her skirt, but was instead dressed in pants and a boy's button-down cotton shirt; she even felt a cap atop her head, which caused her to look up—and that was when she finally saw the man who'd shushed her, silhouetted against the burgeoning candlelight.

Like his fingers, he was long in frame and quite skinny, as if he'd been pulled by his toes and hair until his frame had stretched painfully thin. He had unkempt hair that he may have tried to brush (Dinah noticed a jagged part), although it seemed to spring up at whatever angles it wished and had been further disheveled by the top hat he now held in hand. Like his limbs, his nose was protracted and sharp, but his eyes . . . he had tired, sad eyes—hopeless eyes even. This, Dinah ascertained, was the man represented by the statue and the marker she'd climbed only moments ago.

"I'm afraid you've joined us for our final curtain, young one. Then, we're all finished," he sighed. "Canceled, you know. Aye, how shall we feed our little ones?"

"I—I don't have any little ones," she answered.

"Then, you are my luckiest unlucky employee," he said. "The rest of us scavenge scraps and splats left by our dear patrons. My own Cate was partial to mashed cabbage. But *you* get them all for yourself, lucky devil."

"I'm not sure I understand," she said.

"Who does? Who can? Why must businesses fail? Why must children suffer? Why don't cows eat people? No answers, I'm afraid. No order. No meaning at all. Random, random, random is this life. Don't you agree?"

How ridiculous, she thought, but the more Dinah reflected—on the circumstances surrounding her childhood move to Bizenghast, on sudden bursts of tires, and more recently on absurdly unfair contracts with hidden cemeteries—the more he seemed right. Yes, of course she agreed. Life *was* entirely random. She'd felt that way for years now.

"Actually, yes, I—"

The gaunt fellow turned as more candles cast shivering radiance on stage. In the house, the audience's murmurs amplified, and Dinah thought she even heard something like the sound of chains rattling, of all things. She stepped closer to the stage and saw glints of metal intermingled among the silhouetted heads, arms, and torsos of the crowd. Were they *actually* chained?

"Ah, I've kept them waiting," the tall stranger said. "Hear how they complain!"

"But . . . it doesn't matter, right? If they complain? If you're late? You said it's all meaningless, so . . . so who cares?"

He grinned and tapped his prodigious nose. "Now you've got it. No reason to play by rules when the game has none, I say—except when one *wishes*, of course. And tonight, for once, my wish—my dingy, dark wish—will come true. So hush and get to the ropes. I've packed the house. Tonight's performance is dedicated to my skinny Cate! How she *hungered* for an audience like this!"

"Who's Ca—?"

He drew a watch from his waistcoat and regarded it. "Ah, I'm late—for a very important fate." Gently, he took Dinah by the shoulders, turned her toward the ropes, and hurried to the edge of the side curtains, where he straightened his jacket and ran his fingers through his hair (not that it helped).

Dinah could think of nothing better to do than follow his directions. Besides, she was only here to pull a rope; what was the big deal?

Vincent was missing, and she felt weaker without him. Sure, she could decipher a riddle, and she had proven herself an excellent whiner at the chapel in Maggie Murdoch's woods, but when it came down to the adventures themselves, she *needed* Vincent. He always knew what to do.

She gathered herself, tucked her curls under her stagehand's cap, and gripped the ropes that draped from the catwalks above. Their bristly fibers pricked her palms like needles.

Waiting for the show to begin, she realized something: The skinny man's fingers had smelled strange. Harsh. Like . . . gasoline. No, that would be silly. The people of his time didn't have gasoline, did they?

☽

Until candles brightened the stage, Vincent sensed only two things: one, that he was seated among a good number of people—all mumbling incoherently—and two, that his wrists were bound in iron manacles. He could move his hands only three inches before the chains pulled taut.

"Where are we?" he whispered to a broad-shouldered man seated beside him. He kept his eyes on the now lit stage, wary of whatever might emerge, and counted the rows—six in total between his seat and the main curtains. At present, the stage was set with only a ladder, one enormous enough to reach the top of the proscenium arch.

"Why am I chained?"

Whatever the broad-shouldered man mumbled, Vincent couldn't follow.

"Say again?"

The man repeated himself, uttering a groan once he was finished.

When a baffled Vincent looked up at his neighbor, he immediately discovered the issue: He saw the man's terrified, pained eyes behind an iron mask. The dull, rust-crested mask covered his entire face, from forehead to chin, leaving only eye and nose holes. Painted on the mask was a slapdash happy face. From a distance, Vincent imagined, this man would appear to be having the time of his life.

He turned to look at his opposite neighbor. She, too, wore a mask. Hers depicted a fit of hysterics.

Vincent twisted his body and tried to turn, stretching his fetters as far as he could. The two men behind him bore masks that expressed thoughtful appreciation and deep concentration respectively. And everywhere else he was able to look, masks also covered the faces of the audience members. Sometimes, they dinged and tolled against one another in a kind of discordant melody as the captives struggled for freedom.

The broad-shouldered man next to him attempted communication one more time. "Uff—uffish," he said, his lips compressed against the inside of the iron mask.

"I can't—I don't understand you."

The broad-shouldered man began to cry. Vincent didn't ask him to repeat himself.

An announcer called out from stage left: "Ladies and gentlemen, tonight, we have something special for you: By popular demand—nay, *outcry*—it's Little Charley Lapin's final performance!"

Around Vincent, the audience groaned and pulled at their chains. Vincent twisted and wrenched his own shackles, scraping himself in the process.

A tall man toddled onto the stage, so skinny that Vincent wondered whether he'd eaten in weeks. His stick legs reminded Vincent of the Stiltwalkers Dinah had described to him, although Vincent quickly recognized him as the model for the Mausoleum statue—which meant this guy was important to solving the dream. Good, he thought, that was at least *some* progress.

But where was Dinah? He sought her in the crowd without success. Hopefully, she'd entered this dream in a better situation than he had.

"My dear audience," Little Charley shouted. Vincent determined that Charley had been the one to make his own introduction a moment ago. "Have I got a show for you tonight.

Charley's Last Performance

I daresay I shall *burn* the memory into your hearts and minds for all time." At that, the audience rattled and struggled against their bindings, so loud that Little Charley stretched his frail arms to shush them. "And do you know who you have to thank for it? Why, none other than your own damned selves!" He chuckled and clapped his hands together, rubbing them as if to ignite a fire in the cold auditorium.

"But first, permit me to recite a poem from memory." He paused, clenching his eyes as he struggled to recall. Finally, he gave up some internal fight. "Bother, I seem to have forgotten that one entirely."

Patrons, masked as they were, shouted at him, their voices mixed in fury and terror. "Gyre!" and "Gimbel!" they shouted, crying, unable to utter anything sensible beneath their masks.

Vincent, who remained silent, pressed the side of his face to his shoulder to save *one* of his ears from the deafening clamor.

"Hush, hush!" Little Charley continued from his position at center stage, in front of the very tall ladder. "Allow me instead to recite a poem that I make up as I go. That way, it can't slip my mind."

And this is what he said:

"Child, I see you still, dreaming
Of rivers and queens,
The days were long then.
Pure, fair Cate, 'tis thee I cherish,
Unclouded though thou hast left me, thy
Brow gravely mourned."

His entertainer's grin softened. "How does life jumble so?" he asked the dusty air. "Alas, all's horrid that ends horrid. But did you like my poem? It's an illusion, or an allusion, or likely a confusion, and I suppose that makes it deep, don't you agree?"

"Galumph!" they cried. "Frabjous!" The din magnified until the theatre shook with thunderous, raucous wailing. The captives expected something now—the big finish, Vincent thought—and they tested their bindings with all their strength.

"You're too kind." Mr. Lapin checked his watch. "But—ah! It's that time, oh patrons. You were my royalty, who could not be contented, so I mustn't make you wait."

He took hold of the ladder and began to climb. His legs and arms were so long that he skipped every other rung, resembling a daddy longlegs scampering up the side of a house.

To a stagehand in the wings, Little Charley called, "The rope, please—just a tug. Gentle now, precious!"

A long, bristly rope lowered from the stage ceiling, its end knotted into a noose.

"A snappy end to an unsnappy career!" the entertainer called. "But *hang* on a moment, now, won't you? Hoo-hoo!" Setting his top hat on his head, Lapin climbed the ladder, now to its midway point. "It's time you were 'taut' a proper lesson in courtesy!"

Aggravated by the chains, Vincent found himself shouting on impulse. "No!" He turned around as much as he could, shouting over the crowd. "Whatever this guy's about to do, it isn't good. Do whatever you have to! Get free! Break seats if you must!"

The broad-shouldered man next to Vincent whimpered, shaking his head, though Vincent saw the painted, smiling face more than the hopeless eyes. He couldn't lose hope as this man had, or he'd have no chance of escape.

Charley Lapin turned around on the ladder. "Oh, have we a heckler? Dear boy, you must understand, you are officially my—how many seats does this theatre hold? Ah, yes, you are officially my two hundred fifty-first heckler, which means two things: First, that Bizenghastians have dreadful senses of humor, and second, that I have developed a keen talent for handling your kind. "But what fun would this be if I didn't give you a chance to redeem yourself, eh, young man?" Charley leaned back against the ladder for balance, removing his hat.

"Listen, I wasn't heckling, I just don't like where this is go—"

"Of course you don't. Hecklers wouldn't heckle if they *liked* where things were going, now would they? You really should think before you speak. Now then, here's a riddle—and here's your just desserts if you fail to answer in time."

In a kind of improvised magic trick, Lapin brought forth from his top hat a fresh mask, just like those worn by the other patrons—although this one had been painted to represent weeping tragedy. Once Lapin released it, the mask slowly floated toward Vincent's face. There were bolts in its four corners, which snapped and clanged in and out of their sockets as the mask drifted ever closer to Vincent's face, as if eager to press against his skin and screw through his cheeks and forehead.

Little Charley continued: "Solve the riddle, spare your pretty face. But either way, do shut up afterward."

Vincent struggled against his bindings to no avail. "Hurry then! What's the riddle?"

"A loaf of bread is chopped into three parts. Those three parts are then severed into three parts each, and those parts are hacked into three, as well. With me so far, heckler?"

Admittedly, Vincent's focus was off; the iron mask had already glided across the short span between the edge of the stage and the first row of patrons. Still, the riddle seemed easy enough to follow, and Vincent was decent at math, anyway. "Get on with it!"

"They just don't teach good manners anymore. Fine. Then, those pieces are scored into—" (Here, he paused, perhaps considering a really good number.) "Those pieces are split into one thousand seven hundred thirty-nine pieces each." He chuckled.

Oh no, Vincent thought. He'd rubbed his wrists raw while struggling, and the mask had now passed over the third row— only four rows left! The math had been easy enough until Lapin tossed out that last number. Now, there was no way Vincent could calculate the pieces!

"What's the question? Quickly!"

"The question is: How many loaves of bread do you have now?"

Vincent gasped. "That's it? *That's* the riddle? Give me a break!"

The mask passed the fourth row.

"A simple answer shall suffice."

"It's still one loaf of bread! That's stupid!"

Little Charley touched his stretched, knobby pointer finger to his lip and grinned. "Terribly sorry."

The mask passed the fifth row. Its bolts pulled back into position, ready to dig into skin and bone.

"No! That's the answer. It's fractions. Grade school stuff! It still amounts to one loaf of bread!"

"Your mask seems to disagree. Don't worry. It'll only hurt for a moment. And I can assure you, it's much easier to be an audience member than it is to be a performer—though I suppose this crowd might argue that point."

"Zero? Zero loaves?" Vincent didn't think that was the answer, but he was desperate.

"Uh-uh. Nope. Time to join the rest of my critics."

The mask reached the sixth row. It would arrive at Vincent's row next.

From somewhere backstage, Vincent thought he heard Dinah shout for him, but there was nothing he could do. He *had* to solve this riddle!

Wait, that's it! he thought to himself, drops of sweat falling into his eyes. *This is a riddle, not a math problem.* Somewhere, there had to be a twist or a gag or a pun.

The mask hovered above the seventh row seats, beginning its descent toward his face.

The facts, he thought, *I need the facts!*

Vincent considered as quickly as he could: Lapin has an odd sense of humor. He'd used strange words to describe dividing the bread—

chopped, severed, hacked, and scored . . . so maybe it was more about words than numbers, especially since Lapin had never used the most obvious word when referring to bread, which was clearly—

The mask pressed against his face. Its four bolts began twisting in their grooves, tightening the fit. Just as the pain came, Vincent screamed, "I have it! The answer is: It's still one piece of bread, *any way you slice it!*"

At that, the mask fell to the floor, clanging as it hit the stone and tumbling toward the stage, defeated.

Lapin chuckled. "Not bad! Funny, huh? Here's your victory prize." He pulled a rotten tomato from his hat and threw it; it splattered across Vincent's face and rolled onto his lap.

"Hoo-hoo!" Lapin chortled, and then he continued his ascent toward the swaying noose.

"Oh, that's awful!" Dinah cried when she saw that by tugging the ropes, she'd dropped a noose for Charley Lapin. However loony this man had gone, she knew enough about the Mausoleum and ghosts' dreams to realize that letting a ghost accomplish its "final performance" was a *very* bad idea.

Their job was to break the pattern: to protect the little girl from her homicidal grandfather, to keep the young lord from murdering his lover, to rescue the children from Maggie Murdoch. This time, all Dinah had done was help a ghost along his dark path! And the worst part was that Lapin had mentioned something about the audience playing a role. . . .

Dinah tried to make out the vague lines and shapes of the equipment high above in the catwalks, but the ropes disappeared into shadow—it was simply too dark up there for her to see. She tried climbing the ropes, but the higher she gripped them, the rougher, more splintered, and painful their fibers became. Besides, there was no way of telling how high the ropes went—and in ghost dreams, that meant they could go on forever, for all she knew.

Luckily, not fifteen feet away, and on the same side of the stage as she'd been posted, the manager had left his station and a lantern candle by which he'd been reading. Dinah first checked for other stagehands, who moved about swiftly and silently. When she was satisfied that the wings were clear, she ran to the stage manager's desk to steal the lantern—but not before noticing a newspaper clipping nailed to the nearby wall . . . an article concerning Lapin's show:

"Local audiences at each performance of Little Charley Lapin's Traveling One Man Show always absconded before the curtain, and rightly so—up until his last show. At his final performance, Lapin hanged himself in front of them, prompted perhaps by heavy financial losses and the death of his young daughter, Catherine.

Though onlookers could have left the theatre, they were so transfixed by his public suicide that they failed to notice the doors locking just before the fire started.

Strange, indeed, to think Lapin's show had consistently received high praise in other towns outside Bizenghast."

A fire? Dinah looked at all the candles and lanterns used in the theatre. It would be awfully easy to have a terrible accident here, considering the tall, dry curtains, the ropes, the split-wood planks, and the—what was that scent she'd noticed on Charley Lapin's fingertips? Not gasoline, *oil!* Of course!

She ran, covering the tiny flame within the lantern, until she reached her station by the ropes. There, she held the lamp as high as she could, banishing the darkness. Above, the ropes ran to the high ceiling, where they looped around a pulley toward the front of the stage. Now that she saw the connection between her ropes and the ones above the stage, she understood Lapin's curious scheme: He'd set barrels of oil precariously at the edge of the catwalks above the stage. Once a proper amount of weight pulled on the ropes—say, the weight of a dangling man—the ropes would snap tight, knocking the barrels down toward the candlelit stage and house below. When that much burning oil touched the open flames . . .

"Vincent!" she screamed, heedless of the performance. She *had* to find him, no matter the cost. "Vincent!"

By now, he would've answered her if he were backstage, so she ran toward the doors leading from backstage in hopes of finding him in the house. She found those doors bolted shut—and upon turning around, she found herself surrounded by the other stagehands, who finally revealed themselves.

In the dim, flickering light, she saw that the stagehands—ghosts themselves—had been burned and charred to the point where they moved like voiceless, blackened skeletons, near to crumbling. Two of them grabbed her, one covering her mouth to prevent her from screaming. She could taste the ash rubbing against her lips.

They brought her to the side of the stage, where she would be among the first to feel the lick of the flames. Should they succeed, she knew she'd end up as charred as they'd become.

On stage, Lapin had reached the top step, and he now held the noose in hand. He looked up at the barrels, nodded in thought, and addressed the audience one last time. "Farewell. Farewell to the cruelest town in New England. You ruined me . . . ruined my Cate."

Dinah struggled against her captor. She wrenched at his arm, managing to break free when his dust-and-cinder wrist disintegrated into black powder. She screamed from the wing. "Mr. Lapin, don't! Don't do it!"

"Oh, I'm awfully sorry, my dear, but this is how things go, you know. I'm to bring the house down!" He laughed briefly. "Likely, you've heard that one before. My apologies. You see, extinguishing oneself is dreadfully uninspiring"—he chuckled despite himself—"just ask my stagehands."

More of the stagehands seized her, but as she struggled, Dinah finally spotted Vincent—he was seated in the audience, covered in tomato, bound in chains, and surrounded by people wearing horrible masks.

She had no time to worry about Vincent, though: Lapin had pulled the loop of the noose over his head and was extending his right foot into the empty air. Suddenly, Dinah was reminded of the statue outside this dream realm. Like Vincent, it had been hit by a tomato. . . .

The ladder wobbled beneath the actor. In mere seconds, the theatre would burn to the ground all over again.

"*Here lies me, which is unfortunate,*" Mr. Lapin's marker had read. And what else? "*How about giving me a hand?*"

"That's it!" she shouted. It had been a clue, all right, and not just to give his statue a hand with the rotten tomato. Bound as she was, Dinah struggled until she managed to bring her hands together—and clap.

Hearing her applause, Little Charley grabbed the ladder for balance. He seemed suddenly terrified of the height as the ladder tilted forward onto one pair of legs, nearly tipping, and then leaned back toward the opposite pair.

"What was that? *Who* was that? Who—who did that?" He swung his right foot back onto the ladder, which continued to wobble.

"I did!" Dinah shouted. "I clapped for you! I gave you a hand!"

He found her standing in the wings, struggling against the burnt stagehands. "Oh," Charley said, "that doesn't count, I'm afraid. You work for me. You *have* to clap. So very, very sad. Closest I ever came to applause in this town."

☾

Upon overhearing Dinah's and Charley's exchange, Vincent realized what needed to be done. Dinah wasn't an audience member, but Vincent *was*. Now all he had to figure out was *how* he could he clap, bound as he was.

The answer hit him as tomato guts dropped from the tip of his nose onto his stomach. Quickly, he squished the remaining parts of the fruit toward his left wrist and slathered the manacle, creating a functional lubrication with what Vincent used the call the "boogers" inside the tomato. With one hard tug, he yanked free his hand and applauded, loud as he could.

"Really?" Charley shouted, cupping his hand over his brow to peer into the darkened house. "For me?" He began removing the noose from around his neck, but he lost his balance and fell smack on the stage floor, rolling toward the wings. When he came to a stop several feet later backstage, Little Charley sat up on his boney knees, shaking his head. Already, his form began to brighten, and Dinah knew he would soon be released. But before he left, he saw the little stagehand.

"My little Cate was pretty like you once, before our money and our bellies thinned."

Dinah didn't know what to say. She'd never dealt with somebody else's grief over a death. "Oh?"

"What a strange response," he said, cocking his head as though he hadn't understood her at all. "You might as well say, 'Eee?' while you're at it. It would be equally meaningless as 'Oh?' But then again, what isn't meaningless, eh?"

"I think I agree," she said, disregarding his gobbledygook, "about the meaninglessness—meaning that life is meaningless. It has been for me, too."

Little Charley Lapin looked up. His face beamed with light now. He turned to the audience and smiled, seeing that they, too, were finally free. Their manacles unlocked and popped clean off wrists, ringing like sleigh bells as they fell to pieces; and the masks, tolling the theatre floor, smashed like cymbals and chimes.

"Oh, I wouldn't say 'meaningless,'" he answered. "I don't know about that drivel. I say that there's a lesson in everything, isn't there? Yes. Yes, I think there is. In fact, I hereby announce that there is!" He stood up, his heels lifting off the wooden floor, followed by the flats of his toes.

Dinah shrugged. "Well then, what is the lesson? Please tell me."

Charley began to fly, yet his face remained perplexed. "Oh, I have no idea what the meaning *is*, love," he said. "I only said I knew there was a lesson, not that I knew what it was. Really, you must try to listen better!" Shaking his head and sighing, he flew away, straight through the ceiling, calling for his darling Cate to come to supper.

"I guess you don't want any more studying on the way back?" Vincent asked as they climbed the short ledge marking the end of the Mausoleum and the start of the woods. He'd wrapped his wrists in shreds from the bottom of his shirt and had washed off the rest of the tomato in a puddle by the path.

"Do you ever wonder if this is a dream, Vincent?" she asked.

"This? Right now?"

"All of it, like the way the ghosts live a dream all the time. Do you think I might wake up and find out I imagined all this? Because it's crazy enough."

"I don't know."

"Or what if I thought I were stuck in this lousy contract—right up until some kid came along and I found out that *I* was really the tortured ghost the entire time, finally setting me free?"

"Isn't there a movie like that?" Vincent asked. She said nothing, so he continued. "You ever realize you're dreaming when you're still right there in the dream?" he asked.

"Once in a while."

"For me, it happens a lot. And once I do, I start doing stuff I would never do in real life, just because I know it's harmless. Because I can get away with it, you know? I wake up soon after, but it's fun while it lasts."

"I should try that," she said.

"Well, if you think *this* is a dream, do something crazy right now, right here. Something you'd be too scared to do normally. It would be meaningless after all, right? The whole dream, random and meaningless."

"I don't know," she said. "I'm not so sure anymore. And who could say when I'd wake up, anyway? Or how long this dream will be?"

They stopped walking. He turned to see her face. "So, no?"

"I guess," she said. "I guess it's real." She resumed her walk home. "I'm not dreaming."

She was quiet the rest of the way home, and it was too dark for Vincent to read his textbooks.

VII

THE FOUR GUARDS

*F*unny, the warrior thought, *I don't remember tucking this away.*

He brought his hand to the opposite wrist, where he'd just now discovered a small line of silver hidden among the chinks of his black armor. Delicately, he tugged at the silver, lifting it free as a surgeon might pull a bullet from an ailing patient. There, in the warrior's fingers, was a silver earring.

He held it to his almond-shaped eyes: one silver earring, an inch-and-a-half long, slender and curved, adorned with a simple, gravel-sized cut of aquamarine.

The warrior was alone, for the moment, and seated in his chambers. At his feet were his weapons of choice: the curved Tartar's bow—which he'd been meaning to oil and restring—and his magnificent sword, with its circular, stylized guard, handle wrapped in skin from the belly of a stingray and blade made of white horn. Sometimes, he would spend his time (he had plenty of time to spare, after all) staring at that blade, the way its ivory horn reached like intermingling braids to a striking point so sharp that even his keen eyes couldn't tell when the horn's tip finally gave way to air.

Around his chambers, which were otherwise Spartan in furnishing, were sundry daggers, pikes, and halberds in need of polishing, a marble-hewn chess set (left standing since the last game, which black had won), and gear suited for a life lived simply, far from the pleasantries of civilization. Yet nowhere on his stone floor, nor hooked to the walls, had the warrior kept any elements of protection, for his black armor never came off; the swirled plates and braces spanned from collar to hook-toed boots, and to remove his armor was, to him, as strange an idea as removing one's feet at the end of long day of work.

The silver earring jangled in his fingers, and candlelight glowed at the edges of its stone. "I don't remember tucking this away," he whispered, brushing some of his dark hair from his eyes.

He stood, and his armored body made no noise, so unlike the way a human's steel armor might squeal or ding (not that humans wore suits of armor anymore, which was a disappointing trend). Indeed, as he walked to his door, his boots, although hard and nigh impenetrable, fell as softly and silently as bared feet.

He paused before joining his brother and sisters in the Mausoleum's common area. He would give himself time for this, a moment to remember—it was important to pause, he had observed by watching the humans, before coming to a startling realization. Then, the eyes must flash and widen as the realization came—in this case, that he'd recalled the story of this silver earring.

"Ah, yes!" he whispered, so softly that even brother Edaniel's long ears wouldn't hear him. "Yes! There it is!" He pushed through his mind's memories of the human he once knew—a girl who'd once owned this earring. She hadn't given it to him, but he'd kept it after discovering her remains. Humans did that; they took things to remember, and when they came across these relics later, they remembered, and they cried.

He tried to cry, too. He had taken a relic, rediscovered it, and now he should cry at its significance. He put through his mind the idea that her passing was very upsetting. He understood that it was—he had thought her a very pleasant agent and would have preferred that she'd survived her contract. He closed his eyes. No tears came.

He raised the post of the earring—that part that first tunnels through the ear, before the lever back swings down to secure it—and touched it below his eye. Gently, he rubbed the tip from his eye, down the olive curve of his cheek, and brought it to rest at the corner of his mouth, where he tried to conceive the taste of salt tears. *Yes,* he thought to himself, *that must be very much like sadness. That is what it feels like to cry.*

Now, he tucked the earring deep within a different gap in his armor and tried to forget about it, so that he could be "surprised" the next time he found it. Then, he could discover, remember, and mourn, just like humans did.

The warrior, whose name was Edrear, continued on his path now, entering the common room, where he encountered his siblings gathered before the three arched windows overlooking the yard of their venerable home. Respectfully, he admired the draping heraldry hung over gray walls, marveling at how the glow from the fireplace danced on the shields and crossed swords he'd mounted before departing on his hunting trip. (Actually, he was pleased to see that his brother, Edaniel, hadn't swapped his display for a dirty dinner plate and two large crossed fish. Again.)

Edrear had been off hunting for weeks now, and had only returned on news of recent visitors. Yet as much as he wished to hear of the newcomers, Edrear first bowed respectfully to greet his dear family.

"Grab some bench, stupid," came the reply from his brother Edaniel, who was seated by the fireplace, intently roasting marshmallows, bananas, and a tin can on the end of a stick. "Nobody wants to see your Prince Charming routine."

Eniri, his favorite sister, knelt by the crackling fire, immersed in her work. She'd set before her the jars, vials, and pots of her arcane arts. Breathing deeply, Edrear smelled the familiar odors of his sister's craft: the intimation of herbs like clematis and five-finger grass, and the subtle aroma of burning flesh, probably from the innards of a slithering creature.

Metals and compounds bubbled in the fire while she worked to lay a five-spot on the bare stone floor, carefully pouring salt onto each corner of the symbol. Although she was taciturn by nature (and despite the fact that she barely acknowledged his entrance), she was his favorite among the siblings.

Like Eniri, Endrear was a creature of few words, and they both valued the old ways: Just as he disdained gunpowder and delighted in chivalry, Eniri despised chemistry and adored alchemy. Edrear smiled, knowing she would not turn to see him, but that they would sit near each other later, likely in silence, working at their respective arts. For now, it was enough to see her red hair, tight against the back of her head in twin braids, and watch her shoulders roll as she ground conditioning powders with one hand, and with the other extracted a lizard's kidney.

At her spinning wheel, Elala welcomed the warrior in her quiet voice, tilting her head so that her long, strawberry blonde hair fell clear of her serene gaze. Like his other sister, Elala spoke little; this was good, though, because Edaniel, who was seated on Elala's lap, spoke enough for all of them. Edrear regarded his brother, who was, as usual, in feline form—and only slightly less than usual, covered in melted marshmallow. Well, feline-*like*, anyway, because no stranger who'd ever come across the Mausoleum had ever mistaken Edaniel's pointy-eared, big-headed, spiral-tailed (not to mention *green*) form as a mundane cat.

"Edrear," Edaniel said, barely looking up from his latest issue of *Kippers Monthly* while licking congealing marshmallow off his paws, "I had this great idea to turn a profit on this dump, by converting the Mausoleum into a rollercoaster waterpark. Call it, like, The Waterleum—or Commander Von Slippery's Splash Tomb."

Edrear grinned. About twenty years earlier, one of their contracted humans had told Edaniel that his voice sounded like Groucho Marx with a sinus infection. Edrear hadn't gotten the reference (he kept no television in his room), but his big brother sure went green in the face—greener than usual even.

"I understand we have newcomers," the warrior said.

"More than that," Eniri added, still attending her hoodoo. "We have an agent."

Eniri and Elala

"Wonderful news. But he or she hasn't freed ten ghosts yet?"

"She. No, not yet," his favorite sister answered.

Edaniel slammed shut his magazine and sprung onto all fours. "Keep your Underoos on, Madame Mystico. She'll get around to it eventually."

"I doubt it. They show little promise," Eniri added. This was another reason the warrior appreciated her; she never minced words. She dropped a pinch of powder into a red-hot pot, where it flashed, creating a small, blue-gray mushroom cloud that floated to the rafters. "Hmph," she mumbled, and went back to her work, which Edrear did not pretend to understand.

He looked to his brother for further explanation. *"They?"* Usually, agents worked alone, having been solely bound to the contract. And even if they began with companions, those were often abandoned at the first sign that death lingered all too close in these missions. "Do you agree, brother? Are they lacking?"

"Well," the green pointy-eared monster said, "the agent, she's kinda whiny. You might even say a wee bit grossly and enormously ineffective on a grand scale."

Elala spoke, having been silent at her spinning wheel until now. "Of course, she's at a disadvantage, having been consigned to St. Lyman's all these years. You know how dreary that place is. And I understand she can see ghosts more readily than others. I submit she's progressing well for one who's been mercilessly haunted for much of her life."

"What are their names?" Edrear asked.

"Dinah," his brother said.

"And the other? Is it a boy?"

"Lemme see . . . it's either what's-his-face or Anonymous. I don't know. Larry . . . Octavio . . . who cares? Kid ain't part of the contract—and he'll prolly get himself killed by the end of the week. Death by showboating bravado."

"The boy's name is Vincent, and he's a local. Comes from a wealthy family. They're *old* Bizenghast," Elala said.

At the mention of "old" Bizenghast, Eniri muttered, nodding. She preferred old bloodlines with branching family trees that had grown thick and tall with ancestors; such families kept tradition and ways of the past alive.

Edrear stepped past his siblings and rested his gloved hands on the center window frame. He stared through a clear section of the stained-glass design (this one of a giant brass clock, upheld by merfolk) and inspected the property.

"They're here," he said. "I can see them." The others made no effort to rise. They'd seen this part enough times already; until the agent and her companion entered a new dream, the siblings had better things to do. But for Edrear, this was his first look at the newest agent.

He watched as Vincent, her companion, threw up his arms near the Hooded Angel, complaining, most likely, about having to deposit gold. They *always* do, Edrear recalled.

Next, he turned his attention to Dinah, noting her unusual attire—some kind of overcoat—Victorian, perhaps? Edrear knew nothing of fashion, only that her garments reminded him of centuries past, but he appreciated the memories her dress inspired: recollections of past agents, long since dust, who'd come upon the Sunken Mausoleum. In those days, he remembered, some recruits discovered the cemetery after their horses spooked in the woods, leading their masters right up to the stone arches; others had arrived with leashed hounds, having been led by elusive quarry.

"You don't think she'll make it?" he asked his brother.

"Nah, but it'd be cool." Edaniel hopped off his sister's lap, scampered across the room, and leapt onto Edrear's shoulder. He nodded to their sisters. "You think I wanna watch these two knit and brew funky potions all night? Sheesh, get me outta here, or at least let's get a round of Ricochet Death Frisbee going."

"Soon enough," Edrear answered.

The warrior thought of all the things these humans might learn once they'd unlocked the first of his siblings. Truth be told, there were book loads of things Edaniel and his sisters could tell the humans—like the fact that this Mausoleum was one of many guilds, for instance, or about Bizenghast's longstanding rivalry with a guild in California called The Sulphur Queen. Or Edaniel might tell the new agent about why the Mausoleum was built on this spot in the first place, and how its interior wasn't nearly as empty as she might think, being occupied by a host of other critters, not to mention the Tower Guards themselves. Then, there were topics such as the Messengers, who took newly deceased souls toward the Relays, and even the Hive, which was possibly the single most—

Edrear stopped himself. On second thought, the kids would be lucky if his brother didn't run off at first sight of a good patch of grass. Edaniel was easily distracted by rolling around in the grass. He felt it kept his fur shiny and green. To each his own.

Endrear watched the girl. *Do well*, he thought, pondering that it had been some time since he'd served as guardian to an agent.

Eventually, Edaniel ran off (something about having to write fan mail to Henry Kissinger), and Edrear's sisters continued quietly at their work, with the patience of creatures who will never die and who could never understand the concept of a temporary, fleeting human existence.

So it was that Edrear watched the humans all by himself. He thought of the adventures they might have together once the agent had unlocked his services. By then, the ghosts they faced would be far worse; the agent would need all the help she could get, and Edrear would be ever ready, ever vigilant. It was, after all, why he'd been constructed in the first place.

He watched as they solved that night's riddle and opened the portal into a ghost's dream. He tapped his finger on the window frame in a kind of applause. *One step closer*, he thought.

But from his vantage point, he then determined which ghost's dream they were about to enter, and his enthusiasm waned. A monster lurked in that dream, a formidable one, and it might very well crush the companions. This was the kind of dream he was meant for, but he could not help—not until they'd freed enough spirits and earned his service.

Unable to assist, he dwelled on the idea of the humans failing now, close as they were. When it felt like the right moment, he touched his pointer finger to the inner corner of his eye and traced a line over his cheek, along the edge of his nose, stopping when his fingertip touched his lip. *There*, he thought, the fire crackling behind him, *that's just how a human would cry.*

VIII

THE STALKING SECRET

*D*inah couldn't shake the feeling that they were being watched. She had no more sense of there being spirits nearby than any other night. And as always, when she looked around, she saw nothing but graves and the Mausoleum arches, gates, and statues, quiet as death, just like every other night they'd come. She expected nothing else. But tonight, for some reason, the sensation at the back of her neck had intensified.

"Someday, maybe we should come here in the daylight," Vincent said, "and really look around. There's got to be some stuff that could make this place understandable—clues of some sort."

Dinah sat down, pushing her dress out over her calves for warmth. She concentrated on suppressing the gnawing sensation that unseen eyes were upon her. "What difference does it make? Don't you get it? It's probably not even here in daylight. None of it makes sense—because there *is* no sense."

He didn't answer her. He'd already dropped the second half of his mother's pair of earrings into the receiving bowl, so the doors had opened and were waiting for them to pass through.

"Anything strike your fancy tonight?" he asked. "If not, I found one that we might as well look into." He pointed at the statue of a child covering its mouth. It was diminutive compared to most of the others. "I guess it's as good as any, right?"

"Seems fine to me."

As the statue of the child was only four feet tall, he knelt down to read the inscription:

"Never to talk,
Ever to walk,
Dumb to what I've seen.

At childhood's end,
I'll need a friend
To hear where I have been.

To join the chase
And thus displace
This soul, you must be keen:

Place the husk
That speeds youth's dusk
At feet innocent and clean."

"I don't know if I'll ever get used to this," Dinah whispered.

"Which part exactly?"

"The part where I get stuck saving souls, but in order to do the job we have to give up gold *and* solve riddles. I'm not sure if there's a worse deal in the world than this."

"Maybe *being* one of the lost souls, I'd think. That's probably worse. And not all of them brought trouble upon themselves, which makes their situation sad. But how do we solve this riddle?"

Although she tried not to show it, Dinah smiled. Vincent had asked her how *she* thought the puzzle could be solved. Maybe, just maybe, she'd progressed during her adventures to a point where she'd done at least some of her share of the work; it felt good to see Vincent recognize that. Unless, of course, he'd simply been thinking out loud.

She inspected the statue as closely as possible. As she'd noted, the boy's statue was slight and simple—one hand hung at his side whereas the other covered his mouth, his expression one of worry and pain. At the feet, Dinah noted a short pedestal that rose only an inch or so from the ground, nearly hidden by the long grass.

"Whatever we put at the statue's feet, I bet it goes here," she said.

"Agreed. The question becomes: What's 'childhood's end'?" Vincent asked as he began inspecting the area for clues. "Or, like it says at the bottom, 'youth's dusk'?"

"Something about growing up, maybe?" Dinah wondered. "Love?"

No sooner had she said that than she noticed something glittering at her feet. Leaning over, she dug her fingers between blades of grass and discovered a simple ring. Upon closer inspection, she found the ring itself was quite plain—more like a band, with no mounts for gemstones whatsoever, and no inscription to help guide them, either.

"Look what I found," she said. "It looks like a wedding ring! That works for the idea of growing up, right? I mean, you get married, you have all kinds of responsibilities."

Vincent replied, "Not all of which certain couples actually honor."

"Meaning?"

"To their kids," he answered. "Responsibilities to their kids."

Dinah wasn't sure what to say to that. Surely, he was talking about his own parents again. He might not love them, but at least he *had* them. . . .

In the end, she decided to move forward with the mission. "Well, if this isn't the answer to the riddle, we still have a ring, I guess, right?"

"And if it's gold," Vincent added, "we might even save ourselves some of our own stock tomorrow night. I wouldn't mind that."

Dinah placed the ring on the pedestal. "There you go. Youth's end is when you find love and get married."

Once she'd placed the ring on the pedestal, its slight weight triggered a tiny trapdoor into which the ring dropped. Dinah was close enough to hear the ring clatter within the pedestal, and it reminded her of a quarter clanking through the gears of a gumball machine.

On the outside, the statue of the boy suddenly sprang to life; his one free arm, which had been resting at his side, rattled into action, rotating at the elbow until its hand covered the boy's mouth like the other.

Dinah and Vincent waited for a hole to open in the ground, as usual, but nothing else happened.

"Ooh, that can't be good," she said. "Now both his hands are covering his mouth."

"Maybe we just made this dream a little harder? I mean, we're supposed to 'hear' where he's been, and now his mouth is fully blocked. "

Dinah shrugged. "We'd better not stick any old thing there again; we'd better think it through."

"Right," Vincent replied. "So let's have a look around, because you better believe I'm not dropping any of my own stuff down there. We donate enough to this joint already."

The two began combing the area of the boy's statue. Soon, their feet flattened the grass into a nearly perfect circle, the statue at dead center. Every few minutes, one or the other expanded the radius of that circle until finally they'd discovered several artifacts:

"I've got a pacifier," Dinah said. "Kind of moldy, but hey."

"Check it out," Vincent said. "A torn-up graduation cap."

"Can I have that?" Dinah asked, half kidding. "It might be the closest I get to graduating, the way things are going with Aunt Jane right now." She turned, shaking her head at the thought of staying home from school evermore, and found the handle of a briefcase sitting atop a nearby gravestone. "Here's something, too."

"So, what've we got?" Vincent asked. "A pacifier, which I guess represents having a child. A graduation cap, for education. And you just found a briefcase handle."

"That could symbolize getting a job. I guess they all pretty much have something to do with growing up. The question is, which one do we place, considering that the statue might clam up even more if we're wrong?"

"Well, the marker mentioned something about a 'husk,' so we need an outer shell or something, too."

Vincent looked around one last time, finding a small spherical object partially concealed behind a headstone.

"Hey, cool, looks like a ball of some kind." He walked over to retrieve it.

"Um, Vincent? I'm not sure a ball represents being grown up. It's kind of the opposite."

"So what? Bali-Lali never said we can't have some fun around here while on the job." In the darkness, Vincent jogged to the headstone and playfully kicked the sphere—but he gasped as the top of his foot connected, and even at a distance, Dinah could hear the hollow, hard knocking sound Vincent's shoe made as it hit.

Dinah watched as the "ball" lifted five feet into the air before rolling through the grass like a small soccer ball.

"What the heck was that?" Vincent shouted, hopping on one foot and rubbing his blunted toes.

When the object stopped at Dinah's feet, she leaned down to touch it. The surface was smooth, but subtly grooved where her fingers fell. As she rolled it around in her hands, she discovered two deep sockets and a triangular hole in the center.

Vincent had inadvertently kicked a human skull—possibly, considering its small size, a child's.

Dinah jumped back immediately, stumbling and nearly smacking the back of her head against a grave. Her backside hit the earth, and she scurried crablike away from the thing.

It was more the surprise of seeing the dark, cavernous eyeholes glaring at her that caused her reaction than anything else, so Dinah quickly recovered and composed herself. She'd seen much worse in her young life by now, anyway.

"It's a skull, Vincent. Human. Without the jaw."

"Oh, sorry," he said. "I didn't mean . . ." He trailed off, perhaps wondering whether the skull belonged to someone around there, or whether it had floated out of a shallow grave in a rainstorm or been dug up by grave robbers.

Dinah took a deep breath and lifted the skull in her hands. She stared at it, wondering herself whose flesh might have once covered the bone framing. Could be, she thought, this was the skull of the boy who'd been memorialized here.

"Vincent . . . this is the answer. It's death." She felt herself drifting into her own past, but resisted. "The end of childhood is when you learn that people can die and leave you behind. And the closer death comes, the further from childhood you are. Forever."

She saw that Vincent was about to speak—perhaps to say something kind, albeit uninvited, about her parents—so she placed the skull at the child's feet, causing the hidden trapdoor to yawn open once more. She listened again, this time to the sound of the bone hitting one internal metal lever and then the next, until the skull ultimately banged off one last switch and dropped into the earth with a deadpan thud.

Vincent joined her by the boy's statue, and the two silently waited as the pedestal shifted to the side, revealing a ladder leading down into a cramped hole surrounded by walls of damp soil.

"This poor boy," she said as she accompanied Vincent into the child's dream. "He might have been younger than I was when . . . I had to grow up."

☽

After twenty or so feet of descent, a cool mist enveloped the duo, and soon Dinah felt her fingers and feet passing *through* the rungs of the ladder. First, the sensation reminded her of pressing her fingers through clay—hard at first, but each rung gave way whether she wanted it to or not once the push began. Then, she lost contact with the ladder entirely; she could see it, but not feel it. In the last few moments before she'd fully entered the dream, the mist had thickened so that Dinah couldn't see the ladder at all. She called out for Vincent—and he for her—until they both felt firm ground beneath their feet . . . followed by an unwelcome, saturating chill.

Once the mist cleared, Dinah found herself outdoors, beneath a wooden, roofed bridge, her shoes sopping up cold water from a slow, swirling stream.

Vincent manifested nearby, standing on a submerged and algae-covered boulder. He turned to see Dinah, but as he attempted to get his bearings, he promptly slipped off the slick rock and landed bottom first atop a bed of pebbles.

"Great," Vincent said, splashing as he regained his footing. "We're forced to pay gold for the privilege of risking injury or death on a nightly basis—and *now* my shoes are soaked and my butt's freezing! I love this job!"

Rather than commiserate (which she was tempted to do), Dinah ran to the sandy bank, hoping to beat the babbling water before it completely drenched her shoes and left her shivering for the rest of the mission. Sadly, she was too late; her shoes had sopped up the water, and Dinah could see that even her shoelaces had bloated.

Vincent inspected their surroundings, starting with the bridge. The structure appeared to be intended for pedestrians only. And judging from the dense foliage and trees around them, it had been built out in the middle of a lush forest. He reached up, curled his fingers around a sturdy plank, and pulled himself out of the icy water high enough that he could swing up a leg and climb the rest of the way onto the bridge. "Are you okay, Dinah? I'd offer you my shoes, but we're both—"

"I'll be fine," she said, though her teeth chattered as she spoke. "And I'd offer you some dry clothes, but you might look a little silly in my skirt."

"No thanks." Vincent changed the subject, perhaps trying to take his mind off his freezing rump: "You know what we need?"

"Thermal socks? Rubber boots? Survival knives? Maybe a good rocket launcher?"

"No. What we need—and how—is a guide . . . someone who could actually tell us what the heck we're supposed to be doing, you know? Laying it out, simple and clear. I mean, we spend a good part of the night just trying to find the stinkin' ghost, and then another part figuring out what to *do* about it. By the time we finally get around to solving the dream, it's almost sunrise. What happens if we find one we can't solve in time?"

"Let's hope it never happens."

"But it might—and Bali-Lali said we *have to* save the souls by sunrise. What if we can't?"

"Why are you saying all this, Vincent?"

"Partly because my butt feels like it's going to turn to ice and crack off any second, and partly because we're out in the middle of a forest in who-knows-what time period, we're already running behind schedule, and who the heck knows what we should do now?" Vincent leaned over and pulled a shoe off his foot, resulting in an awful sucking sound, and then he whipped it around, spraying muddy droplets across the bridge.

"Sorry if I made this one harder by giving the wrong answer," she said.

"No, no, that isn't it. That was both of us. But someday, we won't be able to arrive so early. Regular life will get in the way. So, all I'm saying is, wouldn't it be nice if, besides the riddles, we could get a little guidance? Because I bet you ten bucks it isn't always going to be so easy to solve these dreams."

"I don't think it's so easy now."

"And it could just get worse. So, we need a hand here." He pulled off his second shoe, squeezing it over the edge of the bridge. Then, looking up at the sky, he shouted, "You hear me? A hint would be great about now!"

Suddenly, some of the nearby brush rattled and rustled, its branches shaking so that a pair of birds hopped out of the tangle and fluttered off. Then, Dinah saw two small, delicate hands emerge from the thick, spreading leaves and branches apart. A small boy, frantic and nearly out of breath, leapt from the bushes onto the sandy bank where Dinah stood. He saw her and nearly screamed, but he managed to stifle it by covering his mouth with both hands, preventing the sound from escaping.

Evidently, the boy hadn't expected to come upon Dinah and Vincent out here in the forest, so he paused to take a breath, probably wondering what he should do now.

"Hello," Dinah said. She still wasn't accustomed to speaking with ghosts.

The boy had dark hair, nearly jet black. Like Dinah's, his hair grew in curls, though the boy's were closely cropped. His pale face was reddened from a long sprint, and his brown eyes darted back and forth between Dinah and Vincent, as if he pondered who might be the worse threat.

"It's okay," Vincent called from his place on the bridge. "We're friends."

"No!" the boy whispered. "I can't stop. *You* can't either. Run!"

"Run from what?" Vincent asked. He tried to pull his right shoe back on, but it was too tight from the water. "Anyway, we didn't come here to run. We came to help—"

Deep in the part of the forest from which the boy had run, something thumped. Then, Dinah and Vincent heard a second thump, and a third.

A fourth, louder, closer thump followed, prompting the rush of vermin and songbirds to higher, safer branches.

The sequence of thumps were almost reminiscent of human footsteps—but if that were the case, this must've been some *giant* human.

"That's it!" the boy screeched, still trying to be quiet. "It's found me again!"

"It?"

"What's found you?" Dinah asked. She could feel the tiny hairs on the back of her neck standing on end, and her hands began to shake out of fear as well as the cold.

"It," the boy said. "*It!*" Growing frenzied with dread, the boy tried to name whatever followed him. "The . . . the *River Man*. It always finds me!"

"River Man?"

At the sound of two more thumps, Vincent tried again to squeeze his foot into his shoe. Then, from his vantage point on the walker's bridge, he saw the tops of young trees flap side to side like pinball paddles; something in these woods had the power to push trees, and it was fast approaching.

"He's right—something's coming. Something *big*."

Dinah heard the boy whimper. "What is it?" she asked. "We need to know."

The child repeated himself: "The River Man!" Then, he covered his mouth with both hands and would say no more.

Whatever it was, it drew ever nearer.

Thump. Thump. Thump.

Here and there, the thumping, which was surely the sound of its feet shaking the earth, halted, interrupted by a splintering crack, and Dinah could see treetops topple.

Her heartbeat quickened. Her instincts demanded that she find a place to hide right away, and she felt herself backing toward a thick tree stump.

"I have to run!" the boy said. "It's after me! It's *always* after me!"

Thump.

Thump.

THUMP.

Dinah screamed as a creature—nine feet tall or so, by her guess—crashed through the thick brambles and brush into the clearing. Humanoid in shape, as thick as two men across the chest, its arms and legs were as massive as logs. But the strangest part of the monster was this: Its body was made entirely of swirling water, muddy enough to block out what little light had struggled through the treetops; sand swished at its surface, and here and there tiny white waves splashed from one part of its frame into another. Even its eyes were fashioned of water, two tiny whirlpools into which silt and muck curled and vanished.

Despite her terror, Dinah found herself staring into those swirling eyes, which had an almost hypnotic effect. Her heart skipped within her chest, only to rebound a second later, hammering against her ribs. She had seen creatures before—the burnt husks in Charley Lapin's theatre, the dogs with the upside-down jaws—but this monster was giant, and she found in its twisting eyes no trace of thought or emotion.

Her mind drifted to questions of how it might attack her or the boy: Would it cover her mouth with its hand, for instance, loosing a surge of water down her gullet until she drowned here on dry land? To face a raging beast was one thing, but to stand against something so alien rattled her nerves until she, like the boy, wanted only to flee and never see the thing again.

Vincent, meanwhile, had given up on his shoes and ran from his position on the bridge toward the shore, where he leapt at the River Man in an attempt to grapple it. How brave, Dinah thought, but how terribly foolish, too, because Vincent's opponent must have had the advantage of several hundred pounds—maybe even several thousand.

Sure enough, Vincent smacked against the water creature's side, as if crushed by an ocean wave. When he lifted his face, Dinah could see that one side had reddened from the impact. Then, to make things worse, the River Man lifted Vincent in one surging hand and tossed him against a young evergreen tree. All the while, its swirling gaze never left the little boy. It hadn't observed Dinah, and it had dealt with Vincent—but clearly, it cared only about the little boy.

For his part, the boy needed no further prompting. Sobbing, he sprinted deep into the leaves and brush on the far side of the clearing, all the while covering his mouth with both hands.

Vincent opened his eyes and saw the boy running. "He's the one, Dinah!" he shouted, holding his side where it had smacked into the evergreen's trunk. "The boy in the statue! Follow him! I'll try to—" He paused, unsure what to say. Obviously, he couldn't stop this beast from doing exactly as it liked, but he needed to do *something*. "I'll try to distract it somehow. Go!"

Though it pained her to leave Vincent, Dinah turned to follow the racing child.

Intellectually, she knew Vincent was right, of course; if she could manage to protect the boy and resolve his torment, she and Vincent could leave this dream. So, even if she worried about Vincent, the truth was that she might be able to help him most by leaving him behind.

She heard the thumping, the snapping of vines and roots, and the crashing of small trees as the water creature stalked its prey, only footsteps behind. For a moment, Dinah felt relieved that the enemy seemed to be hunting the boy, not her, but she chided herself for such selfishness. If the monster *did* get the boy, Vincent and she would fail. And if she failed . . . well, it was better not to wonder what Bali-Lali might do to them. Maybe Vincent was right—maybe they *could* use a guide.

"Hold on, would you?" she shouted. She jumped over a fallen log and ducked under some low branches that reached into the air like witch's claws. Her lungs ached from the sprint; this path was filled with obstacles—ditches, mounds, thorn patches, and walls of tress too thick for passage—which meant she had to start and stop, leap and land on all fours. This kind of halted running exhausted her more easily than the tracked mile she used to run in gym class, and she winced at the stabbing pains in her stomach and chest.

The boy crawled out from a hollowed stump and turned to see Dinah. "It's no use," he said. "Keep running!"

"How long?" she asked, gasping for air. "How long do we run?"

The boy looked at his feet, holding his sides. "Forever," the boy said. "It won't ever let me get away."

Dinah heard the footsteps thundering behind her. This creature, despite its mass, was fast—maybe even faster than Dinah. It easily pushed aside obstacles that she and the boy otherwise had to overcome.

She watched as it raised a sloshing fist and brought it crashing down on a log, splitting the wood in two. In two steps, it overcame Dinah, reaching the boy.

So near the creature, the boy froze in terror, watching the fluid arms reach out, its fingers extended and aiming for the child's throat.

"I . . . I shouldn't have . . . stopped to talk," the boy whimpered. He covered his mouth with both hands once again.

How odd, Dinah thought, that at a time like this, the boy would cover his mouth. What was he keeping inside?

Dinah screamed as the River Man's murky fingers pressed against the boy's soft neck. Just as it was about to squeeze, Vincent leapt from behind a small oak tree, tackling the monster at its knees (or what looked like knees).

Water splashed to the earth, mixing into mud, momentarily distracting the creature. It reached behind itself, whirling eyes still on the child, and grabbed Vincent, flinging him into the air.

Vincent opened his mouth, gasping and nearly shouting from the shock of falling *upward*. Luckily, just as he reached the apex of his ascent, as he was about to fall, Vincent caught a substantial tree branch to halt his impending crash back to the earth.

"Keep going!" Vincent shouted from his place among the tree leaves. "You can't stop!"

Dinah turned to see the boy, who had already twisted under the distracted creature and resumed his flight.

"Catch up," Vincent said. "We're in his dream. Lose him and we're finished!"

She dug her mud-crusted shoes into the dirt and took off after the boy. "What do I do when I catch up?" Dinah called behind her, her eyes on the forest floor, wary for exposed roots and weeds that might catch her feet.

Dinah listened for Vincent's response, but it never came. *Remember, Dinah*, she thought to herself, *the best way to help Vincent is to help the child.*

With longer legs than his, Dinah expected to catch up to the boy sooner than she did. The child, however, was impressively fast, and he disappeared from sight every so often—this time behind a tree, another moment down in a sloping pit—so that she had to spend precious seconds finding him, never mind pursuing him. Perhaps that was how the boy had managed to escape the River Man all this time.

Looking beyond the boy's direction, Dinah saw a huge break in the canopy of trees. She jumped over a rock, and in the air she saw that the forest gave way to a town.

"Safety!" she shouted. "Up ahead! Safety! There's a town!"

"That's my home," the boy called back, huffing. "I want to go home."

"We can do it!" She hated speaking while running because it broke the pattern of her breathing, but in this case, she felt inspired. Looking over her shoulder, she saw Vincent holding the creature around the neck. He must've fallen onto it after being thrown into the trees, and now he held the elemental as if it were a raging bull.

Even from her brief glance, Dinah had noticed how drenched her friend had become during his struggles. In the dark part of her imagination, she envisioned the creature simply absorbing Vincent into its liquid body; she saw Vincent's hands and face bashing against the creature's insides, desperate to escape and to breathe again, until finally her friend stopped hammering his fists; and his face, now dull-eyed and slack-jawed, slipped back into the muddy water, gone forever.

No, she reprimanded herself, *he'll be fine. We'll be fine. I just have to get this boy to—to do what?*

Dinah turned away from Vincent's battle, facing forward again to see how much closer she was to the boy's town. That was it, she knew—the town was safety. The town was surely part of the resolution to this dream. Even though she'd only looked behind for a matter of seconds, she'd been running at top speed and hence expected to have cut the distance to safety. Funny thing, though: It didn't look like she'd covered any distance at all. In fact, the town appeared farther away than before!

She looked at her sprinting feet and saw that the more she ran toward town, the more her feet seemed to slowly glide *over* the grass and reeds. It reminded her of past nightmares where monsters chased her, and she couldn't outrun them no matter how fast she ran, whether because she moved slowly as if running through molasses, or because her goal always pushed farther away from her, like now. And in her nightmares, when she tried to hide, it only bought her a few seconds, because . . .

Because the monster *always* found her in her nightmares . . . just like this monster always found the boy.

That's what's happening here, she thought: She and Vincent were in a child's dream, and he was having a child's nightmare. Somehow, she realized, she'd have to break the nightmare. But how do you defeat a child's nightmare?

She wracked her brain, but came up with nothing. Surely, she and Vincent couldn't physically destroy this monster—at best, Vincent could hold it off or distract it, and even that came at the heavy price of bruises, or possibly even broken bones if she couldn't figure this out fast enough. So, this fight wasn't about combat prowess.

Then what?

Dinah had no experience with children. In fact, she was typically in this boy's situation—*she* was the one struggling against ghosts and nightmares, with adults coming running to try and help *her*.

Okay then, she thought to herself as she ran, *what do adults usually try to do, and does it work?*

Dinah's stomach turned. She realized she was actually looking at grown-ups like Dr. Morstan as models for how to help this boy. Well, she didn't have any of the doctor's chalk stuff (not that she would spoon that stuff out to her worst enemy, never mind this little boy), but she could—yes, maybe that was it—she could simply try to get the boy to talk about his fears. She remembered Dr. Morstan's frequent comments to her during their sessions: *"If you talk about your fears, you can weaken them."*

Much as she despised the concept of playing the role of Dr. Morstan, that idea made sense in this situation . . . the boy was covering his mouth, after all—she needed to get him to talk!

Although she'd been running the entire time, the town seemed yet farther away. She yearned for its quiet homes and smoking chimneys, imagining the warmth and comfort she and the boy might find inside, as well as the assistance they might receive against this creature, if the people of that town were at all decent. But first, if they were ever to arrive, she needed to weaken this boy's nightmare.

"Listen, you need to tell me what's happening," she gasped, stretching her legs as far as she could to cut the distance. "I can't help you if I don't—"

"I . . . saw . . . what he . . . did!" the boy shouted back between gasps. "But it's a secret! I can't ever tell!"

As soon as the boy uttered those words, Dinah heard the creature groan. Until now, its only sounds had been stomps and sloshes, but the new sound came out like a sickly, deep gurgle.

Vincent hollered from behind, thrashing atop the River Man. "What's happening?"

Dinah turned. She saw that the water creature appeared somewhat smaller now, although it was still a substantial eight feet tall. Even stranger, much of the water had sloughed off.

Actually, now that the creature was composed of less water, Dinah thought she saw something large floating about *inside* the creature's mass. She dared not stand in place long, but she held her position long enough to see what had alarmed Vincent: a purplish-white body floated within the monster!

Dinah watched its limp hand and wrist flop to the surface of the River Man's thigh, only to drift and sink again inside the thing's shoulder, near Vincent's shocked face. From its neck, she saw a hip and thigh splash and vanish, hidden in the depths of its watery chest.

"Whatever you did, keep it up!" Vincent cried. "It's shrunk! You've uncovered something!"

Encouraged, Dinah turned to catch the boy, nodding at Vincent to save her voice and breath for the mission. "We can't keep running!" she said to the boy. "Running away gets us nowhere!"

"It keeps me alive!" he called back.

Dinah felt a pang inside her; she knew the boy was long since dead, probably murdered by the stalking River Man, and it hurt to see that he hadn't understood his own demise. But there was simply no time. There was never time to mourn or to cry—or even to think. Vincent had been right about their fight against time; like him, she began to question how long the two of them could hope to enter these realms and send spirits to rest before some clock halted, marking their first and last failure.

"Do you want to live your whole life running away?" she shouted. "Try to trust me. It's the only way."

The boy simply covered his mouth with both his hands again.

Dinah remembered dropping the wedding ring at the boy's statue, and how that had caused the second hand to cover the boy's mouth. It appeared that she'd accidentally made this dream a little harder by making the wrong choice earlier. Thank goodness, she consoled herself, that they hadn't made any other wrong guesses.

Well, if the boy was going to make this harder, she'd have to be a little tougher, too. Her thighs and calves burned, but Dinah ignored the pain and pushed forward as fast as possible, grabbing her quarry by his damp collar. She turned him around, his feet slipping into the air from his halted momentum before smacking back onto the soil.

"Listen to me!" she shouted, although the boy was merely inches away. "Has that ever happened before?" she asked. "Has the River Man ever shrunk before?"

Fearfully, the boy glanced at the oncoming beast. "No. Now, please, we need to run!"

"No," she said. "We can't run forever. We'll never win that way. You said you had a secret."

"Let me go!"

"Tell me more of the secret and I will." The boy tried to struggle away from her, ripping his shirt.

Now that his skin was exposed, Dinah could see that the fair flesh around his neck darkened into blue-black rings. She winced; that must have been how the boy had died so many years ago. Whatever was following them now had caught him and strangled him.

She searched the area for a hiding spot and found a series of hewn logs. Partly to comfort the child, partly to keep him from escaping and running endlessly, Dinah held the boy at his bicep and pulled him behind the logs.

"It'll find us here," the boy said. "It *always* finds me."

"I know. I've had this kind of dream, too. We need to hurry, okay?"

"Dream? This isn't a dream. It's real!"

She had no time to explain. Besides, how could she get a child to understand that fears and nightmares are more sophisticated than they—

She stopped herself. If she said much more, she might actually start to sound like a clone of Dr. Morstan, and there was no way Dinah was going to let *that* happen.

She heard crashing as the River Man neared, as well as the sounds of Vincent struggling against its pounding fists. In seconds, the creature would loom over the logs and grab the child, murdering him a second time.

"Time's running out," she said, "and I'm not going to let this continue. You *have to* tell me!"

"I was only out for a swim," the child said. "I didn't mean to see."

"See what?"

The River Man roared in the distance as though pained. *Good*, Dinah thought. She peeked into the space between two logs and saw that the creature had been reduced in size again. Now it looked more like a bulky man than a creature composed solely of river and mud.

The thing that had been shifting and moving inside the River Man also had become more clear: Pressed against the elemental's physique, curled over its shoulder, was a female body in a soaked and filthy dress. The female—clearly the thing

Dinah had seen washing about inside the monster earlier—was half submerged on the River Man's torso, as if she'd just washed ashore. Perhaps *she* was the secret . . . although there was clearly more to learn.

The monster turned to run at the boy, but Vincent kicked its knee, bending the joint in an unnatural direction. It bellowed in pain, yet remained strong enough to turn and punch Vincent so hard that Dinah screamed at the sight of it. Vincent fell backward, knocked unconscious.

He had expended every effort to help Dinah and the boy, and now the rest was up to her. She was, as she had feared to this point, *alone.*

She checked to see how far they were from town. She could see the bricks of the chimneys and the shingles of roofs from here, and even the frames of windows. They were closer, she was sure of it, and Dinah hoped that maybe, just maybe, they could actually reach sanctuary once the boy had broken down more of the nightmare.

"The secret," she said. "You need to tell it to someone. It isn't a good secret, and it's been hurting you as long as you've been keeping it. Tell me. Tell me, and we can get you safely back home."

"He said that I can't ever tell!"

"Who said?"

The boy turned and saw the River Man storming at them, now merely the size of a tall adult, but only thirty feet away. It moved slowly, hefting the weight of a soaked corpse and walking with a limp, thanks to Vincent's kick.

"Him! *He* told me I could never tell!" The watery creature convulsed, more water dropping to the floor.

Dinah turned and saw that town was closer still now: She could see door latches and window dressings, even names of businessmen like blacksmiths and glassblowers painted on signs swinging in the breeze. What's more, she saw the silhouettes of people milling about behind curtains and dimly lit windows. She pulled the boy to his feet and began running again, giving them a little more distance, a little more time.

"You're doing it!" she said, trying to keep her voice cheerful despite being terribly worried for Vincent. "Do you see? You've made the River Man weaker!"

She took his hand, and they ran into town, the boy screaming all the way. When they reached a well, Dinah saw that dawn had just reached its pink fingertips into the sky; the sun would soon rise. In the homes around them, candles flickered to life and eyes peered through windows to see the source of the noise.

By the time the River Man had reached them, nearly a dozen of the town's men had come out from nearby shops and homes. Responding to the boy's screams, they'd brought the tools of their trades: pitchforks, knives, axes.

"Finish it," Dinah said. "Say the rest. It's time to stop running."

The boy hadn't seen his town in what must've felt like forever to him. Somewhere nearby, his mom waited for him, and his dad was already up and tending to the animals on their property. He would be able to see them again, finally. He could see his parents and feel safe at long last.

The boy turned and pointed at the soaking creature. "That man!" he said. "Mr. Jacobs—he killed Mary Whitmore by the bridge! I saw him do it, and he came running for me! Mr. Jacobs choked Mary Whitmore to death!"

At that, all the water rushed from the River Man's form, leaving only an aging, miserable-looking Mr. Jacobs—holding the dead body of young Mary Whitmore in his arms. With the disappearance of his swirling eyes, so went his great strength: He dropped the dead girl's body right in the center of town as yet more of his fellow citizens stepped from their homes to see.

"Please," Mr. Jacobs said. "This is a mistake. I merely . . . found her."

Dinah feared the people might believe him, but the boy ran forward, pulling at his collar.

"And he choked me because I saw!"

That was enough for the men of old Bizenghast. Dinah rejoiced to see that the boy began to glow a soft, brilliant white as he ran, skipping toward his home, shouting for his parents. And as the dream began to fade, she heard the satisfactory ringing of metal as the irate townsmen made a circle around Mr. Jacobs, their axes and knives and pitchforks raised, their knuckles white, their eyes grim with violent planning.

She exited the dream as Mr. Jacobs grunted. And though she shielded her eyes from the gruesome sight, she heard the distinct sound of a cleaver—chopping at spare ribs.

"Are you sure you're okay?" she asked.

She'd helped Vincent all the way home, him limping with his top half leaning over for most of the trip. He'd made every effort to hide his pain, which troubled Dinah; she couldn't tell how bad off Vincent actually was.

"The worst part is that I really liked my shoes. And now, who knows where they are."

"You're being macho."

"What kind of macho guy says he misses his shoes?"

She laughed despite her concern. "I guess they're somewhere in the dream now."

"But hasn't the dream ended? What happens to them once we've accomplished our mission?"

Dinah shrugged. "Maybe we'll find your shoes outside, by the Mausoleum's entrance somewhere. I like the idea that the dream is over, though—as in, a dream doesn't have much purpose after it's done its job of scaring you, or trying to tell you something."

Vincent paused. He tried to look her in the eye, but it was difficult to stand straight. "Maybe even the scary dreams are just trying to tell us something."

They reached the point of the path where the woods met the road toward town, and here Vincent straightened himself, ignoring the pain. Dinah wondered whether it was Vincent's pride; maybe he wouldn't allow himself to look undignified where other people could see him. She guessed really rich people might be that way.

"So, how'd you end up making the creature shrink?" he asked.

"I made the boy tell his secret. Made him talk. That made his fears go away."

"Nice. How'd you know to do that?"

She didn't want to tell Vincent that she'd learned it, in part, from having to meet with people like Dr. Morstan. She hated that she'd taken anything positive away from her times with him; to her, it was like solving one nightmare with another.

"You know I have a lot of bad dreams," she said. "I guess you develop a talent for nightmares after a while."

On her insistence (and after much protesting on his part), they reached Vincent's house first. She assured him that she'd be fine the rest of the way home, and that she wasn't frightened; after being chased by a murderous water creature, a bump in the night held little power over her.

"So, you better sleep in your real house," she said. "Not in your backyard home."

"That *is* my real home," he said. "But fair enough. You're sure you'll be okay?"

"Don't worry about me," she said. She looked at him—how desperately he tried to appear as though he were perfectly healthy and uninjured, even as he winced while reaching for the doorknob.

"Guess what?" he said, opening the door. He appeared embarrassed at being escorted home by Dinah, but he smiled nonetheless. "Tomorrow, I think we're both going to be absent from school."

She could hear his unsteady, pained footsteps as he climbed the staircase.

Returning home, she feared for a day when he might try to face too large an enemy. What would happen then? Would she be left alone, truly alone—forever?

Vincent was right—they would need help at some point, because if they didn't get it, someday either she or Vincent might step into a dream and never step out.

IX

THE WILD BEAST

"*A*re you all right?" the voice asked.

Dinah couldn't identify the speaker; she'd been sleeping too soundly when the voice began speaking, and her brain was still trying to fall back into slumber. All she managed was something like, "Mnuh?"

"I said, are you all right? How are you feeling?"

Now she could tell it was a male voice. Perhaps Vincent had come to visit. She hoped he had. She hoped he'd healed overnight and had come to show her how much better he was feeling. *It could happen*, she thought. *In dreams, anything can happen.*

"Vincent?" she asked. She opened her eyes and found that she was facing her wall and window, away from the source of the voice.

"I'm afraid not," he said, and now Dinah knew that Dr. Morstan was speaking to her.

She turned under her bedsheets and glared at him, testing her vision and her mental clarity to see whether he'd drugged her with the chalk stuff again. She could see him clearly, the afternoon light reflecting off his glasses, and her mind recalled immediately just how much she disliked visits from the doctor—which at least meant she hadn't been drugged yet.

"Why are you here?" she demanded.

"Another visit. Routine, except that Aunt Jane informs me you continue to sneak out at night."

Dinah said nothing. In her opinion, no good came from speaking to people like Dr. Morstan. He would simply turn her words against her and make a note on a pad that sent people to take away her life and freedom.

"Do you care to share anything about that, Dinah?"

"No."

Dr. Morstan sat on a chair next to her bed. She could smell his aftershave; it made her nose twitch. He placed his notepad on his lap and slapped his palms against his knees. "You know, I'm very worried about you . . . about you placing yourself in dangerous circumstances."

Before she could think about it, she blurted out, "I don't place myself in dangerous circumstances. Other things do."

The doctor reached a finger up to push his glasses high on his nose. His eyebrows lifted; now he was getting somewhere. "Tell me about these other things, Dinah—these things that place you in dangerous circumstances."

"No."

"Why won't you?"

"Because you'll turn it against me."

"I'm not your enemy, Dinah. I'm here to help you. That has always been my job."

She stared at the ceiling.

Dr. Morstan continued. "These 'other things' that place you in dangerous circumstances . . . is one of them Vincent Monroe? Does *he* place you in dangerous circumstances?"

"No!" she shouted, her gaze meeting the sunlight flickering on his eyeglasses. How dare Dr. Morstan make such a suggestion! "Leave Vincent alone! He's helped me more than you ever will!"

"How so?"

"It's none of your business."

Dr. Morstan took a deep breath and squinted his eyes. "You know, you aren't helping yourself. Going out at night, accompanying this boy to who-knows-where . . . acknowledging that you are encountering dangerous circumstances."

"I didn't say that—you did!"

"But you agreed, Dinah. You only differed in that you absolved yourself of blame. But you agreed that you are in danger, and *that* is a concern. A very grave concern."

Dinah sat up. All the sleep had left her. She felt her pulse throbbing at her temples and wrists. Her forehead had moistened, and she felt weak—worse than weak . . . pathetic. She had seen monsters and ghosts, had struggled against them, and yet this man—this ignorant doctor—terrified her, not because of who he was, but because of what he could do to her.

"You're going to . . . you're going to do something about me, aren't you?"

Dr. Morstan rose from the chair and looked at his notes. He flattened his lips as though he'd just arrived at very troubling news. "Do you know how your actions have contributed to this scenario, Dinah?"

She felt the urge to roll off her bed and hide beneath it. This man could have her taken away—away from Vincent, away from her aunt, away from school and the shreds of life she grasped for dear life—such as the illusion that she might be allowed to return to classes and be a regular girl. But this man had power over her. Real power. There wasn't anything she could do against him, and that idea terrified her.

"Please don't send me away," she whispered. She'd never pleaded with him before because she despised his visits, but now she was like an animal in a cage, declawed and dependent on a master's whim. "Please, please don't."

Dr. Morstan walked to her bedroom door. He held the frame as though bracing himself. When he turned to her, he had a practiced, clinical, emotionless expression. "I'm going to do what I believe will help you."

And that was that.

Dinah slumped in her bed. It was only a matter of time, she knew. Someday, she would roll over in bed again and hear whispering. She would awaken, and they would take her away, hands on her shoulders and wrists, hands against her back to urge her into an idling van. She would be tucked into a room where doctors watched her through cameras and small glass squares in reinforced doors. And if Vincent or Aunt Jane ever came to visit, she would find that there was little to discuss, because they lived in the real world, and she in the white confines of instituted respite.

"Are you resting well?" they might ask, and Dinah saw herself picking at jagged fingernails, staring at corners.

"I am, and they treat me very well here," she might say, because if she told them the truth, that she was screaming on the inside, Vincent and Aunt Jane might decide that next Sunday would be better spent *not* visiting Dinah, and she would be forgotten.

It was only a matter of time.

☾

That evening marked the hardest decision she'd had to make concerning her visits with Vincent to the Mausoleum. On one hand, Aunt Jane had informed Dr. Morstan of Dinah's nightly escapades, and Dinah had seen clearly that Dr. Morstan was on the brink of making his final assessment. So, to leave again meant Dinah was essentially asking for the psychiatrist to make the worst possible conclusion.

On the other hand . . . what would happen if she *didn't* go? Dinah never forgot the image Bali-Lali had presented when Vincent asked why they should bother abiding by the contract: Dinah's own corpse, gray and wilted. How could Dinah refuse the Mausoleum when all signs pointed to the dismal reality that her very existence was in peril?

So it was that Dinah had crept out of her bedroom long after Aunt Jane had fallen asleep watching late night talk shows. Down the road, she'd found Vincent waiting, and from there they'd trekked together to the Mausoleum.

Now they found themselves inside another ghost's dream, having solved a simple riddle that required them to find a secret door fashioned within a nearby tree. This dream reminded Dinah of some of the previous dreams that had taken place in the deep woods of Bizenghast, and she wondered how they all connected: When in time was Maggie Murdoch compared to the River Man, for instance? Were the witch and the murderer contemporaries? Or had the psychotic grandfather and his granddaughter lived around the same time as the young lord who'd slain his lover or Charley Lapin, who'd burned a theatre to the ground? Someday, she thought, it might be interesting to fashion a timeline of all these lost souls, to see where (that is, *when*) she and Vincent had been. Someday . . . assuming she wasn't bedridden all day and running for her life all night, that was.

She and Vincent crouched once more among thick, ancient trees, this time overlooking a small old-fashioned town. This settlement was smaller and simpler than the River Man's, and Dinah thought it might have predated the setting of their last adventure. She mused on the possibility that the quiet boy's great-grandparents were running about as children somewhere in this dream, which begged another question: When did it start, this spiritual restlessness in the town of Bizenghast? Did all cities and towns have some kind of Mausoleum, or was Bizenghast especially cursed? She could believe the latter was true, judging by the town's economic downturn and its general state of rot—but who really knew? Maybe she was one of many kids stuck with vile contracts issued by spider-ladies. Maybe even spots like Cape Cod had a Mausoleum (likely right on the beach, where the ghosts wore sweater vests). So many mysteries, and no way to solve a single one . . .

In the dark, she checked on her friend's condition. "You feeling better?" she whispered.

"Much," he answered. "Only a few scratches. Nothing worth discussing."

Vincent leaned from behind an oak tree to study the town. His shirt pulled up as he leaned, and Dinah noticed some bandages wrapped around his side.

He continued. "It's funny. This town looks like a smaller, older version of the town we were in last night, with the River Man."

"I thought the same thing. That it's further along in the past."

"Could be. I mean, aren't we always in some version of Bizenghast when we go to these dreams?"

"I'm trying not to make sense of dreams," Dinah responded. "Not much point. We can make up all the theories in the world, but we'll never know—not if things stay like they have been, anyway, with us running around clueless."

"Well, we may as well start heading toward these folks if we're going to find out what we need to do tonight."

With that, they began a slow, careful walk down a woodsy slope, careful of any mudslides or gatherings of pebbles from old riverbanks (or from riverbanks that didn't exist yet, though the thought made Dinah's head spin). Vincent kept an eye on the tall trees, and an ear out for any kind of critters that might surprise them; but happily, the journey to town was easy, quick, and free of stomping giants. The rest of the mission probably wouldn't be nearly as easy.

Near the outskirts of the settlement, but still within the safety of homes, Dinah and Vincent found a group of teens—two girls and a boy—standing in a tight, almost conspiratorial circle. The girls wore odd white caps that reminded Dinah of the old folded hats nurses used to wear. Their dresses were deep red—or brown (it was hard to confirm in the dim evening light), and their aprons matched the brightness of their caps. The boy wore a simple cotton top, pants, and leather boots with shiny buckles.

"I think they might be Puritans," Vincent said. "We studied them in—" He paused. He hadn't meant to remind Dinah about her absences from school anymore. "I know a little about them, and that kind of looks like how they dressed."

"As long as they're not going to attack us on sight, I'm happy," Dinah said. "My feet are still sore from last night's chase."

Considering what he'd learned about Puritans—that they were a tad jumpy about things like witches, for example—Vincent was less relaxed than Dinah. Maybe, *hopefully*, they weren't Puritans after all, because he could envision a stern, gray-haired Puritan judge looming over Dinah, accusing the strangely dressed girl of witchcraft and demanding that she be thrown in the river to determine whether she was the Devil's thrall. It was one thing to study about people in textbooks and another thing entirely to walk among them in dreams (not to mention risk being hanged by them). The bottom line was that he had no way to confirm his anxieties, and only a few hours left in which to help whatever restless ghost lurked nearby.

From their vantage point, Dinah and Vincent heard the teenagers talking, especially as the three seemed to grow excited by the conversation:

"I saw it crawlin' along the hillside last night," the boy said.

One of the girls—the black-haired one—added, "An' meh brother saw it run up a tree, quick as ye please!"

At that, Dinah and Vincent turned to inspect the trees surrounding their hiding place. Satisfied that "it" wasn't above them and about to pounce, they returned their attentions to the teens.

The boy slammed his fist in his palm. "S'only a matter of time 'til it gets in the sheep pen ag'in."

At that, the lighter-haired girl, who'd been pulling absently at her long braids, gasped: "Mercy, no!"

The teenaged boy backed up a step and changed his tone so that he sounded more in control, more like an adult. "Just you wait....We'll get a couple o' men together. Tonight's the night ... that hellspawn's goin' back to the Pit for sure."

Vincent sighed. Yup, they sure sounded like Puritans. All he'd need to confirm it would be a minister's speech about everybody burning in hellfire on God's whim. Even without that, he was pretty sure he was right, which meant somebody was about to get hanged, drowned, or crushed under stones. Yippee.

Dinah patted Vincent's shoulder. "Whatever we have to do here, it must have something to do with the men going out tonight to hunt this thing."

"You're probably right," he said, masking his concern. "I wonder if it attacks them. We should—"

Vincent paused mid-sentence. Beyond the fair wind rustling the young leaves overhead, he could have sworn he'd heard something—something close, hurrying on foot. He held a finger to his lips and gestured for Dinah to come close and listen.

That was when she heard it, too—footsteps, light and swift.

Vincent looked up at the evening sky and saw a shape—about his own size and build, but wild-haired and silhouetted against the crescent-mooned sky—leaping from a tree down to the grassy earth. It dropped effortlessly, and with such grace that Vincent knew it hadn't suffered any injury at all from the height. Then, as soon as its feet touched the ground, it compressed its knees and launched into motion again, bolting deeper into the woods—directly toward Dinah and Vincent!

It smashed into Vincent, knocking shoulder against arm, and Vincent caught its face for only a moment—it was human, certainly, but with untamed eyes flitting this way and that like an undomesticated beast's. The young savage gasped as it hit Vincent—alarmed to have banged into someone out here in what the Puritans considered the Devil's country. It sprinted away, as graceful and focused as a hunted deer, and within seconds, it was gone, deep in the woods and away from town.

Vincent held his upper arm, which had taken most of the impact. "Who the hell was that?"

Dinah had no answer; she looked fearfully into the woods, and then at Vincent's newfound injury—another bruise to add to a growing list.

"Come on," Vincent said, resigned. "Let's meet some townspeople." He wasn't in love with idea of walking into a Puritan town as strangers (and in the middle of night), but there seemed no other option for learning about the scenario he and Dinah faced. They walked to the edge of town and stepped over the rough line that indicated the divide between civilization and that other, frightful realm known as the natural world.

"How many times you think we'll do this?" she asked.

"Do what?"

"Walk from ghost woods into ghost towns, like we're the sheriffs in these here parts."

"Got me."

"And will it ever get to the point that we're no longer afraid? Where *I'm* not afraid, at least?"

Images of court proceedings and nooses flashed through Vincent's imagination. He'd read *The Crucible* just this year with Mr. Wickershire, and he knew how bad this mission might go. Sure, he knew that they were a people who'd fled England for religious freedom, and that he was probably being biased . . . but hell, they killed people they thought were strange, and the intricate dresses Dinah wore each night—well, they weren't exactly Puritan chic. "You're not the only one who worries, Dinah," he said, leaving it at that.

For her part, Dinah lifted the bottoms of her dress as she stepped over a muddy path and enjoyed the older architecture of the homes. These were structures of stone and wood, with exposed beams crossing in large Xs along the exterior of the buildings. Dirt paths stretched from home to home, connecting and leading toward the center of this small settlement, made by the constant plodding of thick shoes.

On occasion, Vincent and Dinah passed hurrying locals, though few paid them much mind as yet; it seemed that anyone who was out this late at night was on a mission, and that mission began at the center of the settlement—so that was precisely where Dinah and Vincent headed.

Once there, they saw men carrying homespun weapons—torches, rakes, and the like. There were a lot of them out there, ready for whatever battle awaited.

"Where's everyone going?" Dinah whispered.

Vincent decided it was time to make contact with one of the inhabitants, much as he would have preferred not to. On the other hand, the sooner he knew what the trouble was, the sooner they could solve it and escape the dream. He stopped a woman who was busy running food to her husband. "Excuse me, what's the fuss about?"

The woman was in too great a rush to pay much attention to them. She barked out her answer while holding a cloth over what smelled like freshly baked bread. "About?" she hollered. "Why, we're goin' to catch that demon in the woods. He's a blight on this poor town!"

She must have seen how clueless the strangers were because she added, "Years ago, the Devil took an orphan boy from the town into 'is lair. Out in the woods he lives now, doin' Satan's work. At night, he creeps into town, steals our poor animals . . . eats 'em right there in the pen, and runs away! 'Hides,' we call him."

Vincent, aware of how much time they'd already spent trying to discover their mission here, turned from the woman in a rush; more than ever, he wished Bali-Lali would just issue them a memo or something for each dream, allowing them to do the job faster and easier. But no, apparently it was better to pay gold, fret over riddles, and waste precious time figuring out their purpose.

"Dinah, I think this Hides fellow is our target."

"A feral child," Dinah whispered. "The poor thing."

As soon as Dinah expressed pity for the wild boy, the woman stepped closer, as if to inspect her. She hadn't paid them much mind until then, but the more she noticed Dinah's strange attire, the more her eyes darkened with grim understanding.

"Here, you know the beast? Why is that?" the woman asked accusingly.

At this, a man stopped his preparations and walked behind Vincent. "Their clothes are strange to me—*and* their faces."

Before Vincent had a chance to ponder what the man meant about him having a strange face, more of the townspeople had gathered. Whispers swept back and forth among the crowd, followed by angry suspicions as to the strangers' purposes here. Finally, the man who'd questioned their clothes and faces, who must have had some authority in the settlement, shouted, "Tie them up, quick now."

The men did not hesitate to grab Vincent at the collar, and Dinah watched in dread as her friend was yanked off balance, backward into the crowd. What was worse, she knew Vincent's myriad injuries were more severe than he'd admit, and that he couldn't possibly stand against this large a mob.

For whatever reason—perhaps because she was a lady—they'd grabbed Vincent first and fiercely, but not yet Dinah. She ran backward several yards, her attention focused on her friend. "Vincent!" she shouted as some of the group broke off to deal with her.

"Dinah, run! Find Hides! Make him leave the woods before they kill him!"

"Stop her!" shouted angry voices from the crowd. That was enough for Dinah. Her biggest fear in every dream thus far had finally come true: This time, she was completely on her own, without her companion to help her at all. And she would have to find a feral boy—and convince the wild child that he needed to leave before the mob killed him . . . and possibly her and Vincent, too.

She tore through the woods, her body better acclimated to athleticism due to her nightly adventures, yet her dress snagged on shoots and bramble, tripping her unless she raised it to her shins. *Why oh why did I wear another dress?* she scolded herself. If she survived until dawn, Dinah swore she'd ask Aunt Jane for track shoes, gym shorts, and maybe a good Swiss army knife. (This was an entirely sensible idea, though sadly, she forgot it three breaths later—running from a mob has that effect on one's memory.)

She struggled to keep her senses keen, although the speed at which she ran rushed blood past her eardrums, weakening her sense of hearing. She ran deeper, deeper into the dark wood, her eyes watering from the winds, her ears catching only the breeze, her blood, and a single owl's hoot as she dashed past the creature, its yellow eyes terrifying her.

She ran, deeper into the night and into the Devil's realm, as the locals had called it, until she lost her way and couldn't tell one tree, one path, one cluster of stones from another.

Then, as she reached a clearing, the blood still dashing at the walls of her skull, she halted. Behind her, she heard shouts and screams for revenge and cleansing . . . but here before her, the feral boy had landed from the shadows of tall trees.

Dinah held her position, gasping for breath, as Hides stood on his feet, watching her as a rabbit watches a child who crosses its path. *What will the human do?* the rabbit seems to wonder. Just so did Hides wait and watch, sniffing the wind that blew at Dinah's back.

They stood for a full minute. Slowly, Hides began to relax in Dinah's presence. She found him easing his limbs—and at one point, he even scratched his cheek with an impossibly sharp fingernail, as if wondering what a creature like Dinah was doing so far from her human world of metal, fabric, and fire.

She whispered, "Please don't be afraid," but her lungs had not yet recovered from the run, and she coughed as she tried to speak. At this, Hides crouched on all fours, ready to spring away—and in fact, he hurdled into the thick, up the side of a tree and deeper into the woods at a speed that Dinah couldn't hope to match.

"Ah! Hey, wait!" Dinah shouted, though she tried to keep her voice directed away from the hunting mob and their torches. "I have to tell you . . . wait!" She ran a few feet toward where she'd last seen Hides, but he was gone.

"Please wait!"

Back in town, Vincent was having a bad night.

Some of the locals—older men, zealous youths, and angry wives—had stayed behind to take care of the stranger who'd stepped forth from the unclaimed and uncivilized woods, which God and Man had not yet conquered back from the hands of Satan himself. This oddly clad stranger seemed to know too much about the evil, feral child, and as far as the people were concerned, it was high time they purified the land of this newfound malevolence.

Vincent struggled, but he couldn't avoid the overwhelming grip of the masses, nor could he prevent them from slinging a thick noose over his head and tightly around his neck. His only relief was that Dinah had escaped—for the moment, anyway.

"Hey! Get this off me!" Vincent shouted to apathetic ears. "I'm not a witch!"

One of the elders approached with a cold fire in his eyes. "Y'are, I say! Suckled on the teat of the Evil One!"

The crowd shouted in agreement, lifting Vincent onto a wooden crate. Once Vincent was standing on the uneven construction, two boys maneuvered the other end of the noose over a sturdy bough in preparation for a hanging.

There, by himself and without much hope, Vincent watched the angry crowd. Even their children were among the onlookers, eager to see a witch get his harsh comeuppance.

"*Suckled on the teat of the Evil One?*" Vincent thought to himself. *That's just gross.*

☽

Once more, Dinah ran as long as she could. All the while, she sought the wild-haired feral boy the locals called Hides, but she turned up nothing. She lacked the numbers that the mob would use to surround and snare their quarry. Worse, Hides outclassed her in terms of knowledge of the land and raw strength; it was simply impossible for her to keep up with someone who had lived virtually his entire life struggling against the rigors of the natural world.

Thus, she found herself in the middle of the woods, out of breath, under the moonlight, near a solitary oak tree. Hides was long gone, and she expected—actually, began to hope—that the mob would find her, because if they didn't, she would be lost in these woods without hope of success and resolution of the ghost's dream. And that kind of failure likely spelled doom for her and—*Vincent. Oh God, Vincent!* What might they have done to him by now? She sobbed at the thought; she had been her friend's only chance at rescue, and she'd failed.

"It's no use," she said to no one, deep in the woods. "He won't listen!"

She had failed.

Her fears came flooding at her. What would failure mean to Bali-Lali? What might be the punishment?

And if she *did* survive the Mausoleum's reprimand, it was only a matter of time before she faced a nightmare in her normal life, too: Dr. Morstan was going to take her away, she was sure of it.

"How can I get him to listen?" she shouted. She waited, crying for herself and for poor Vincent, who'd suffered beatings in order to give her the chance to succeed, and who was now caught by an angry mob who would likely kill him simply for being different.

Nothing answered her. Hides did not return out of sympathy. She would receive no breaks here. She had failed, and now . . . now it was time to give up hope.

She leaned against the large tree and waited for something to happen—anything: for the mob to find her and carry her off . . . to wake up back in her bed, having discovered this was a nightmare or that she truly was insane, just like Dr. Morstan suspected . . . to return to the Mausoleum, where Bali-Lali might open one of her ceiling hatches and pull Dinah up and inside by her hair, delighting in the screams and the desperate thrashing . . .

Dinah heard a creeping, "shushing" sound coming from the tree against which she leaned. Then, something touched her pointer finger—and as she looked up, other things brushed the rest of her fingers, and then her hand. Branches . . . tiny, vining branches had sprouted from the tree to ensnare her, and before she could pull away, they had her by both hands. Next, the branches clambered over her wrists and up her arms, where they reached across the open air to grab at her face and wrap around her neck. She struggled, but it was a fight against strong, living wood, and she could not win. By the time she attempted to scream, stems had already reached out like tossed ropes, catching her around her mouth, stifling all sounds. Then, as she watched, the trunk of the tree opened like a cavernous maw, and her vine-covered body was tossed inside, like a casual snack.

This, Dinah thought, struggling against the mouth, fighting for life against the crushing trunk-jaws of the great tree, *this is death. This is my punishment for failure. And fittingly, it's as random and pointless as my life has been.*

And the process of her demise played very much as the rumors went concerning death. She *did* see her life passing before her, but only selections . . . only moments she would rather *not* have seen:

Headlights rushing toward her parents' car, her mother turned, smiling at Dinah, ignorant of the next second's impact . . . Dinah powerless to prevent the crash . . .

Struggling against the Governess in her bedroom . . . powerless against the cold grip of that wicked specter . . . powerless to convince Aunt Jane that their house was haunted . . .

Touching the black key in the Sunken Mausoleum . . . powerless to avoid condemnation to service . . .

Staring at her own dead body, presented by Bali-Lali . . . powerless to resist such a monster . . . powerless against her own terror . . .

Powerless against her aunt, who had authority over her . . . powerless against Dr. Morstan, who would manipulate Aunt Jane until she agreed to doom her only niece . . .

Powerless.

Powerless.

Absolutely *nothing* in her life was by her decision. She had no control.

The tree's jaws crushed Dinah's body. And as she squeezed into a tight ball to steal a few gasps of life, the tree relaxed its joints, resting for the final compression. When Dinah felt it mashing her again, she knew this was it: the end.

This was life: powerlessness in the face of life's assaults; powerlessness against the crushing jaws of this tree.

And then, even as bark squeezed her ribs ever tighter, and even as she felt her collarbones bending to the breaking point, she closed her eyes and stopped being scared. At first, she hadn't intended to stop being scared . . . but once she stopped, it was infectious.

Well, fine, she thought, *let's end it here.*

She was going to die. Fine. No point in being scared.

Or maybe, if she *did* survive this, Bali-Lali would attack her. Well then, Dinah realized, Bali-Lali would, and it was as simple as that, and there was no point in being scared about that, either.

Or the spider-creature wouldn't attack her, and Dr. Morstan would send her to the loony bin. Also fine. Sure, none of it was under her control, but . . . it was high time she stop being scared.

This place was a dream, and she was tired of being afraid of dreams. She opened her eyes. *Enough,* she thought to herself. And then, aloud, she called out: "Enough."

She felt the pressure ease, and she pushed with her legs to rise from her collapsed position. She reached her hands out and pressed against the tree bark, not so much with her muscles as with her will. And as she pushed, the tree gave way until it split—and she stepped out of it, free.

She saw two things upon her emergence. First, she had been physically transformed by her battle with the great tree. She and Vincent had sometimes experienced such magic in the past—for example, having been made young—but here, she had melded with Nature itself, so that her dress had become lush with vibrant green leaves.

She was *alive*.

Moreover, her very flesh had taken on the strength, tenacity, and beauty of the bark, so that she appeared as a dryad, a creature she'd read about as a child—a fay creature of the woods, bonded to nature, to the seasons, to the trees themselves. She was, by her own observation, as much a being of these woods as any creature of the animal kingdom, and as divorced from the ways of humanity and these Puritan settlers as the surrounding flora.

Good, she thought. *I'm different . . . and I have been for a very long time.*

The second thing she noticed upon escaping the tree was Hides himself. The feral child had returned to her after all, and he was kneeling at the place of her attack and eventual reemergence. In his earth-rubbed hands, Dinah spotted one of her hair ribbons, which must have fallen off during the struggle; she watched him sniff it as he knelt before her new, resplendent form.

She had been through much by now, yet this new confidence—this new strength—took her by surprise. She spoke with authority that startled her, yet she embraced it. "Can you understand me now, Hides?" she asked, already knowing he could.

He stared at her in wonder, and she reached out for him. More than ever, she felt connected—connected to dreaming, to life—and strong enough to separate herself from what pained her.

"This is no longer your home," she said to the feral boy. "Home is now far away, over the mountains."

The boy's fear had left him; Dinah's confidence and assurance had washed it away.

"You understand the trees and the rocks," she said. "Can you understand that you're free now?"

He stared at her, reaching one dirt-encrusted hand up to touch her face. She let him. She understood him as a fellow outcast, and in that she found their bond. She understood him, and he understood her as a fellow outsider.

Hides stood, turning to face what Dinah guessed was the direction of the town one last time, and then he sprinted into the night toward distant mountains, where he would finally be safe from the bloodthirsty settlers.

Now, she knew, it was time to rescue Vincent. As she began her flight back to the town, she felt her form returning to normal. Revived, she ran in the direction Hides had faced. It occurred to Dinah that she might have misinterpreted Hides' glance, and that she might be running into the night, farther away from Vincent—but she wasn't afraid. There was no point at all in being fearful anymore.

Happily, Hides *had* indicated the right direction back to the settlement, and Dinah made quick headway toward the town center, shouting as she ran, "I did it, Vincent! Hides is gone! He's gone away to the mountains!" She stopped to take in new air. "He won't be back. . . ."

She stopped in shock at the edge of the town square, where she found a huge crowd surrounding Vincent. He was seconds away from dropping and swinging from the tree, his feet convulsing and kicking at the air.

Vincent grinned, seemingly oblivious to his dire circumstances. "Hello Dinah, have you met the mob?"

From behind, one of the men kicked out the crate from below Vincent's feet. Immediately, Vincent fell, his eyes wide with shock.

No! Dinah thought, *not after all I've done!*

She shouted at the peak of her voice: *"No!"*

And in that instant, light burst through the dream until the settlement faded from her eyes, and she found herself back in the Mausoleum, with Vincent safe and sound next to her. He took no time in pulling off the noose that would've snapped his neck in another instant.

"Well, that was a fun crowd. Last time I ever buy fudge from the Amish!" There probably wasn't any proper connection between the people he'd just faced and the Amish (Vincent was pretty sure there wasn't), but it didn't much matter. He'd almost been hanged as a witch, and frankly, he was pissed.

Dinah was the first to look around. They were indoors this time, back in the familiar setting of the Sunken Mausoleum, but . . .

Together, they gazed upon a new doorway, one they'd never seen before.

The top of the portal was over ten feet tall. At its peak, the black iron gateway had a clock without minute or hour hands, and the only Roman numerals listed were IV and IX. At either side of the doors were bas-reliefs of mermaids, their tails high in the air as they played harps so well molded as to appear pluckable. Two crafted compasses, one on each door, lay melded beneath iron grates that hinted at the dark passage beyond this gateway.

It was there now, but it had never been there before—of that, both Dinah and Vincent were certain

"Does it look a little different in here?" she asked.

"Oh, maybe just a bit," Vincent answered. "Though I can't imagine what gave it away. . . ."

X

THE ANGEL IN DISGUISE

*T*he companions stood before the newfound portal for nearly ten minutes, lost in their own thoughts and in the detailed iron workings of the gateway itself.

"Where did these doors come from?" Dinah asked, knowing Vincent had no answer. It seemed the only question she could bring herself to ask . . . the only question that mattered to her at the moment. The manifestation of this structure meant that someone or something had chosen to place it here, and she wondered why. Had she and Vincent cleared the cemetery of its lost souls? That would be great news—yet she doubted that were it, as she'd seen night after night just how many tombs, graves, and markers awaited.

But if they weren't finished, then what was this door about? A reward of some kind for rescuing as many souls as she had? A punishment of some sort from Bali-Lali for a mistake they'd unwittingly made? Dinah felt herself growing nervous at the idea, but she held firm to her newfound strength; whatever this gateway meant, she would accept it as bravely as possible.

Vincent murmured a response to her question. "Where does anything come from around here?" He pointed toward the center of the doors, where words had been inscribed in poetic form.

"Read the plaque," he said.

Many lost souls need salvation's light,
Many do not deserve it.
Some cannot find a path through the night,
Some must find a way to earn it.

Twenty black windows look into the cold,
Behind which no remains are interred.
Twenty blue glass panes hold evil untold,
A careful, wary hand is preferred.

Twenty white portals show the blessed undone,
Who lack courage a pathway to find.
Blessed are they who uncover each one,
Free each spirit, each soul, and each mind.

But for those who are few, against ours so many,
A guide can be given to aid these.
A light in the tomb when there might not be any,
And a friend to help others find peace.

Seek to give hope where there was none before,
Free up the souls of imprisoned two score.
To summon Edaniel at the door,
Knock once, then twice, then twice once more.

Again, they stood hushed by the enigma before them. Dinah wondered what all that might mean, her eyes returning to the ending lines about summoning this "Edaniel" person. She covered her mouth with her hand, pondering the poem.

"It can't be that easy," she said.

Always a man of action, Vincent shrugged. "I'm knocking."

And he did: once, twice, then twice once more.

In that moment, the door creaked open, and a creeping, gray mist seeped into the room, enveloping at first the floor, then the spaces at their knees and waists, before finally eddying at their heads and higher, so that they nearly lost sight of the doorway.

Dinah grabbed Vincent and he held her; she had no intention of getting separated in this chaos.

"Oh my God. . . ." she gasped.

"Get down!" Vincent shouted, his attention fixed on the ceiling.

Dinah watched shadows drip like ooze from the ceilings down the walls, forming skulls and spiral spines. Within these demonic figures, spaces cleared of ink so that the thick shadows appeared to possess white, ominous eyes that glared at the shivering youths.

As Dinah and Vincent were surrounded now by mist and shadow, they could not decipher the location of the abrupt, booming, shrill voice that echoed: *"Who calls upon the first of the tower guards?"*

Embracing, Dinah and Vincent had no answer; the engulfing dark magic and wicked phantoms had stunned them into silence. They clung to each other, anticipating the arrival of a magnificently horrific creature, wondering what it might choose to do to them.

But just as the youths had closed their eyes, unwilling to see the source of the bellowing voice, they heard a paltry "poof" behind and below them, followed by the pungent smell of sulfur, which Vincent would later liken to a fart.

"*Kazam!*" shouted a creature as it appeared in the smoke. Then, quieter, it added, "Nah, go on . . . I'm just playin'. Silly kids."

At the mention of "silly kids," Dinah opened her eyes to see. Once she looked, her anxiety left her, replaced by curiosity, for she saw a small, outlandish critter, about the size and shape of a common house cat. But it *wasn't* a cat at all, she knew, because it looked like no animal she'd seen before. In fact, it barely looked *real*. True, it had paws and a long, curling tail—and yes, it had eyes, a mouth, and ears, but the creature looked more like a construct of sorts than anything. The more Dinah looked at its diminutive form, in fact, the more she considered that if she'd seen its face in a storefront, she wouldn't think she'd just seen an animal for sale; rather, she would have believed some craftsman had fashioned a mask of some tribal trickster, hewing it with exaggerated, sharp features. Its eyes were half moons set like gems into its face, without any kind of fleshy hollows or edges, as one would expect from a living creature. Its ears stood like skinny triangles or radio towers atop its head, and its teeth . . .

She stepped away from Vincent. She needed to *really* examine this creature. Its teeth were triangular, like its ears, but they sat perfectly in the critter's perma-grin mouth, so much that she wondered whether the teeth were separate units, or whether it simply had one giant tooth with jagged magic marker delineations meant to suggest many teeth.

"Who are you?" Vincent asked of the creature.

"I'm teacher certified," it answered.

"No, you're not!" Vincent called back, his fear gone

At that, the greenish creature, which one could only classify as Some Kind of Pointy Monster, leapt onto Vincent's shoulder, its paws snug on the boy's collarbone. "Oh yeah, buster?" it nagged, its curled tail twirling behind it. "That's for the state of Massachusetts to decide. Are you the governor? No way, not with that haircut."

"What?" Vincent appeared as if he were starting to regret knocking on the portal.

Dinah approached again, and the miniature monster hopped off Vincent, back to the floor. "We . . . we thought you were another one of those—"

"What," it replied, cutting her off, "another Bali-Lali? That dame's totally square. Her and the Cleaners are a buncha—"

"Cleaners?" Vincent interjected, only too happy to interrupt the rude little bugger. Vincent noted, with some bewilderment, that the faux feline had somehow manifested a little hat while it spoke—a hat reminiscent of Abe Lincoln's, except that it had a tiny flower tucked into its band.

The pointy monster jumped back onto Vincent, this time on top of the boy's head. As quickly as it had made the hat appear, it caused it to disappear, and Vincent began to wonder whether this new arrival was being molded from magic—if magic really existed.

"Yeah, Cleaners, I said it. You won't meet *them* unless you screw up big time. Nasty things. No social breeding. And don't get me started on the Secret Santas we have around this place at Christmas. If I get one more box of dead roaches as a gift, I'm out."

By now, Dinah's curiosity (not to mention her patience) had reached its breaking point. "Who *are* you?" she demanded.

"Keep your skirt on, sister. I'm getting there."

Again, the creature seemed to work a bit of sorcery: It made a book entitled *Mausoleum Employee Handbook* appear out of thin air—in addition to a new hat, which looked strangely like a minuscule snake wearing its own Lincoln-esque hat. If the pointy monster *were* conjuring these things magically, it was doing so quickly, so quickly that Vincent couldn't tell whether it made things appear or had simply been hiding the props behind its back.

The creature read from the employee manual. "'Greetings, my name is Edaniel.'" At this point, it looked at Dinah and Vincent, as if for a reply. Getting none, it sighed and went back to reading. "Edaniel. Edan-yull. E-dan-yell. Gosh, that's hard to say." It continued, inserting little asides as it read: "'I'm the first of the four Tower Guards'—well, *duh*—'that you must unlock before your tasks within the Mausoleum are complete,' etc., etc. 'You must unlock all four Tower Guards in order to gain the experience and wisdom'—well, I don't know about *that*—'wisdom required to complete all of your tasks'—boy, this thing repeats itself a lot!—'within the Mausoleum.'"

"Wonderful," Vincent said. "Another obstacle."

Edaniel chimed in. "Nah, I'm like one of them Cracker Jack prizes . . . the *good* kind, like army men or decoder rings—not this whole paper-tattoo-sticker crap they're doing nowadays."

Dinah looked at Vincent. Vincent looked at Dinah. Together, they looked at Edaniel, incredulous and increasingly underwhelmed.

Edaniel paid their puzzlement no mind and continued his Cracker Jack rant. "I almost choked to death on a Dick Tracy watch once. In retrospect, I should not have eaten it, box and all. But the bottom line is that *communism is bad for your eyes.*"

The pointy monster waited for a response to this insanely deep insight, but the two children said nothing. Finding no reply, Edaniel seemed to suddenly realize his apparent error: "I mean *television.* I get those confused."

There, that was better. Now, surely they'd understand how keenly shrewd he could be. Unfortunately, the boy moron didn't see things that way. He reached out and grabbed Edaniel by the scruff.

"You're a lunatic."

Edaniel, now wearing a lovely pink bow stuck at the base of his triangle ear, wiggled in the air, trying to get free of Vincent's grasp.

"You're cute! Now clam up. I ain't finished."

The Tower Guard squirmed out of Vincent's grip and hopped back to his trusty book, where he thumbed through the pages so fast that they blurred in Dinah's vision. "Uh-huh," he said, "Sleep and Confusion . . . yeah, did that . . . okay." He found his proper place, closed the book, and for some reason

Vincent no longer cared to ascertain, Edaniel decided to stand atop his manual like a pedestal as he spoke, gesturing to the two humans as if addressing an audience of thousands. "As the first of the Tower Guards, it's my job to help you with your duties in the vaults. I can't fight your battles for you, but I can give you information about what to do. I can also stay handsome and witty in the face of danger, which is more than I bet either of you could manage."

"That doesn't sound helpful at all!" Dinah exclaimed. She sat down on the floor in a huff, feeling totally betrayed. Her hopes that this so-called Tower Guard was going to help them were rapidly vanishing.

Secretly, Vincent disagreed. As he'd mentioned in an earlier mission, he believed they *did* need a guide. The thing was, he certainly hadn't envisioned a guide as snarky and altogether annoying as Edaniel was proving to be.

Edaniel strutted toward Dinah, throwing his shoulders in a way that reminded Vincent of John Travolta. "Well, that's why you need the other three Guards, genius! *They're* the ones who can fight! You get a new Guard when you complete ten vaults. Ten more after this and you'll get my brother, which is reason enough not to go on. Welcome to Wet Blanket City, population *him*. But at least he knows all that martial-artsy weapony stuff the kids are into these days."

Brother, thought Vincent. *A brother who can fight?* Vincent felt a strange, sickly clamminess itching up his back as he heard that. He'd been doing just fine protecting Dinah. "We don't need him," he said, crossing his arms. "We've done just fine so far."

The Ghostly Vaults

"Says you," chuckled Edaniel. "What with the hangings and the guns and the tomatoes in yer face. The first ten are the easiest, ironically. The farther in you get, the more vicious the spirits will become."

Suddenly, Dinah shouted from her place on the floor. "*Why?* Why do we have to do this? I haven't slept in days!" She sat up, and Vincent thought he saw all her frustration from over the course of these nights, all her exasperation and anger, boiling from her darkening eyes and dour brow. "We're tired!" she shouted, squeezing Edaniel's fuzzy stomach and shaking him as though he were a cheap, plush stuffed animal one might win at a carnival. "We're sick of coming up with gold tolls every night! *Why us?*"

Edaniel slipped out of her grip, flipped backward in the air, and landed on his hind legs, all while somehow wearing a fedora that had appeared—well, out of nowhere, just like most of what the green rascal managed.

Edaniel raised his paws and shouted right back at Dinah: "Because life's not fair, woman! And maybe because you trespassed here first! Maybe because of a lot of stuff about fairness I don't have to explain because this isn't an after-school special! And F.Y.I., your friend there doesn't have to keep coming back."

"What?" Vincent asked, staggered. The very idea that he'd leave Dinah to go it alone in this insane place was both insulting and shocking.

"You heard me, Frankie. There's no contract with *your* name on it. You're free to go."

"But . . . my arm . . ." Vincent recalled the day he'd found the mark of the Mausoleum inked on his forearm. He'd taken that as a sign that he'd been bound like Dinah, though informally, to the nightly tasks, contract or no. "The other day it—"

Edaniel finished Vincent's line of thought: "Showed the Mausoleum's brand. Only because you helped Dinah. It won't reappear if you stop coming back." He crouched on the ground and grinned while digging his claws into the floor, as if immensely pleased with himself.

Vincent couldn't bear to look at Dinah; he couldn't imagine how she might take that news. "I'm so confused," he said.

"Of course you are," Edaniel said. "Grab some bench and let me explain—wait, hang on." He busied himself with a fluffy, heart-printed pillow and a fez cap (and a medium Coke, and a toy mouse, though Vincent tried to ignore them out of respect for his own sanity). The pointy monster proceeded to fluff the pillow until it was just right, and then flopped onto it. "I like to be comfy in the midst of long, convenient blocks of exposition," he said casually, pausing once more as if expecting some unknown response from either human.

Dinah wasn't sure what he was always waiting for them to say; she almost felt like chiming in with a "you don't say!" or "how amazing!" just to placate him, but by the time she thought of it, he'd already moved on.

As the companions listened, Edaniel cleared his throat, hummed to warm his voice, and then began his tale.

"The Sunken Mausoleum . . . this place is a place where restless spirits are stored until they can be processed. You should realize by now that not everybody dies happily or peacefully. Life is full of pain, and sometimes that pain stays with you even after life.

"Ghosts are a nuisance on the collective unconscious of the world. They're like static on a radio. They accrue and interfere with the living. They're confused versions, nightmares of their former selves. It's the Mausoleum's job to collect the restless ones, process them, and then pass them along to the next world. Without us, life on this planet would grind to a halt."

Vincent glanced at Dinah, who was transfixed by these revelations. Even he had to admit that Edaniel, annoying as he was clearly going to be, did seem to know what he was talking about. Like it or not, Vincent had gotten his wish for a guide.

Edaniel carried on. "We have sixty vaults available for storage ... only forty are occupied right now. Each vault holds a spirit, and each spirit is asleep. Ghost dreams aren't like living dreams. . . . The living rarely dream of reality, but the dead think of nothing else. Cold, inevitable reality. Whatever reality they had in life that caused them so much trouble gets imbedded in their dreams, then twisted and turned around into something awful."

Edaniel paused to take a drink through his straw and motion with one paw, indicating he'd moved onto a new subject.

"The sum of the Mausoleum's staff, as it were, is made up of a head manager, a staff, and a cleanup crew. The Hooded Angel is the manager, the Tower Guards are the staff, and Bali-Lali and her crew of Cleaners are caretakers. But we're all spirits, every one of us, made from remnants of other people's souls.

You'll meet my brother Edrear next, and then my two sisters. We can't interfere with the dreams of other spirits without the help of the living. That's why we employ human agents to do some of the work."

Edaniel winked at Dinah, who did not at all appreciate the effect.

"That's where *you* come in. Once we get human agents, they have to go the rounds and clean out the vaults—solve the ghosts' dreams. If they succeed, they get a big fat reward at the end. If they fail, they get assimilated into the Mausoleum as one of the Cleaners."

On this point, Vincent had to butt in. "What the hell is a Cleaner?"

"Hang on," Ednaiel said. *"Cleaners!"*

The Tower Guard watched the ceiling, so Dinah followed suit. As she watched, a ceiling hatch opened. She expected Bali-Lali to emerge, until another ceiling hatch, and another, and another opened, clanking and screeching. Before she knew it, nearly a dozen hatches had released, and she watched as a multitude of spider-creatures dropped on lines from the forty-foot height to barely four feet over her head.

"Oh my God!" she screamed, covering her eyes. "Oh God, no!"

She had found bravery, true, but seeing these pathetic creatures—multi-limbed and agonized, with ribs that broke through their flesh like daggers, with tongues dangling, eyes and mouths missing or twisted, and all their mangled bodies attached by hooks to the Mausoleum itself—seeing these creatures and knowing that she might *become* one of them horrified her, because it was surely a fate worse than death.

"Yup," chimed Edaniel. "Cleaners. Defilers of the Mausoleum, trespassers, vandals. . . . We don't tolerate disrespect. We're kinda picky like that. But we do offer a 401(k)."

Vincent, too, had lost his courage in the face of these sad, tortured figures. "And we're . . . going to become those . . . ?"

Whether Edaniel hadn't noticed the companions' despair or simply didn't care was hard to say. Either way, the Guard answered, "Not necessarily, chum. It's *her* contract, after all."

Now that Vincent had his answer, Edaniel waved his paw. "Cleaners, get lost!" Straightaway, cords and hooks wrenched their wretched forms into the secret passages, where they disappeared. Then, Edaniel turned to Dinah, who was holding herself for comfort.

"You know, you and what's-his-name here *could* switch. Give him your contract, and you're free to go. If you're into that kinda thing."

This revelation took Vincent by complete surprise. "We're allowed to do that?"

"Sure. It's a free country."

Seeing his friend in possible shock, Vincent ran to her and held her. Her flesh was freezing to the touch. Her flesh had gone pale. He *had* to help her. "Dinah," he said, "You hear that? You're free to go!"

She seemed to awaken from a dark dream as he said the words. "You . . . you mean it? You'd do it for me?"

Of course, he thought. *Of course I would*. He thought of his family, looked at Dinah, and knew that this would be a noble path, a path that could save his ailing friend. Horrible as it was here, he would be willing to take on her contract.

"Oh, Vincent!" she shouted, roused from her grief. She embraced him, holding him tighter than she ever had. "This is the first good thing that's happened to me in weeks!"

Edaniel, not so savvy when it came to sensitive human moments, reacted to Dinah's newfound energy and busted out his own form of joy. Filled with an unheard rhythm, he shook his tail, waving his arms in the air. "You bet it is!" he shouted. "It's electric! Boogie woogie woogie!" He began a mad caper about the floor that was no doubt meant to show empathy with Dinah's sudden happiness, but in reality looked more like he had an itch on his back that he couldn't quite reach.

Vincent did his best to ignore his esteemed guide.

Dinah's grasp on Vincent loosened. She pulled herself away, downcast. "But I . . . no. No, I can't. I can't leave you to do this all by yourself."

Vincent pulled Dinah close to him. He admired her reluctance, but he contemplated all the times he'd had to calm Dinah as the ghosts of St. Lyman's School for Boys tormented her. He recalled her dizzy, blank expression each time Dr. Morstan had drugged her. No, she couldn't do this alone. It would only destroy her. And having seen the price of failure, there was *no way* he'd let her suffer eternity as a Cleaner. No way.

"Dinah, listen to me," he said, his hand gently touching her hair. "You're not well. And I can handle this better than you can. I want you to go home now, and forget all about it."

He tried to see her eyes, but she kept her face buried in his chest, concealed.

How could I refuse? she wondered. Vincent was the closest thing to a hero she'd ever known, and she believed he'd have an excellent chance of accomplishing the task of freeing all the Mausoleum's ghosts—especially now that they were beginning to unlock the Tower Guards. He was right—she *was* sick. She couldn't fulfill this contract, could she?

She wanted to lift her head and look at Vincent. She wanted to nod and allow him to take on this burden. But something stopped her.

What was the problem? The choice made *sense*. Her life had taken one horrid turn after another, and finally—finally— someone had offered her a gift that could truly help. Dinah thought about it: If she didn't have to spend every night rescuing ghosts, she could actually get some sleep and stop upsetting her aunt by sneaking out. By not sneaking out, she might be able to deter Dr. Morstan's decision to hospitalize her, because he'd see that she was making positive efforts. Plus, she'd already grown from her adventures . . . she was stronger now, and she thought she might be able to handle the hauntings within her home. And if she could do *that*, she might be deemed cured—and resume normal life again.

It was perfect.

But she couldn't accept . . . partly because she cared for Vincent, certainly. But perhaps more important, because she'd come so far in these past nights . . . and as much as she might not want to admit it, it was because of the trials she'd faced in the Mausoleum. Yes, it was a horrific place, and yes, she would face ever-worsening dangers in the nights ahead—but it was *her* place, in a sense. And every time she resolved a new dream, she'd come away better for it.

She'd spent her years seeing life as random, pointless . . . she'd called it a die roll and assumed that on some cosmic level, she must have rolled snake eyes. And that had been damned convenient, because it permitted her the right to crawl into a shell and raise the white flag, blaming the whole thing on someone else.

But in these past nights, Dinah had walked in the dreams of the dead. She'd watched them come to peace, saw the imagery of their angel wings, felt the warmth of light and watched fear give way to peace. In this Mausoleum, with its enchantments, and in the dreams she'd entered, she couldn't be sure whether there was actually a system in effect that proved life had some unseen order to it, after all. She couldn't know for sure, but she could at least say it was possible.

Yet even that seemed less significant now. The world might well be pointless. And what if it were? She allowed herself to assume it followed no rules and ran by utter chaos. So what? That was the *world*, not her. Dinah didn't control the world, but she could control herself for a change.

She'd been bound to an arbitrary contract. Fine.

She could evade it, hiding under her bedsheets and sipping chalk dust.

The Dreams of Ghosts

No. No more. She lifted her chin and met Vincent's gaze.

"No, Vincent. It's my contract. And I'm going to stay with it."

She felt his shoulders drop, his arms slacken. She withdrew.

"I just . . . I just want you to be happy," he said.

"I'm tired, Vincent. I'm tired of being scared all the time." And then, with a tone inviting no dispute, she said it: "I'm staying."

Behind her, ever the breaker-of-moments, Edaniel made a bunch of sickly gagging noises before adding in a kinder tone, "You're sure of that? We'll be glad to have you aboard, little missy."

"I'm sure," she said. "Let's go."

XI

THE LIGHT IN THE STORM

Unbelievable, Jane Addison thought. The girl had gone out again.

She stood in the doorway to Dinah's room and pulled her robe tight around her chest; the old home's heating system was touch and go, and tonight's weather had turned particularly sour. From her place at the door, Jane watched lightning strike somewhere in the woods of Bizenghast, and she waited until she heard the rumbling thunder.

Did she really go out in this weather?

What could make her niece want to run off every single evening, especially in a rainstorm of tonight's magnitude? The impulsive, easy answer seemed to be Vincent, her boyfriend, or whatever they were calling each other nowadays. But that felt less believable; Dinah saw Vincent during the day, and Jane hadn't forbidden his visits, so why should Dinah run off under heavy rains to rendezvous?

Jane thought of Dr. Morstan. He'd been a companion and a guide through this mess of parenting, but lately . . . well, the more she thought about sending Dinah away, the more Jane felt like a failure. She hadn't asked for this turn of events. She hadn't asked for parenthood, hadn't desired the role until later in life, if ever—so what harm was there in allowing someone to take away her burden? It was perfectly fair, all things considered. She supposed that was why she'd agreed to a new test with Dr. Morstan and a second, more experienced doctor, this time at the sanitarium itself. Dinah was going to hate her for that, but what options did she have?

There *must* be something else going on, she decided—something larger than Vincent Monroe. And if Dinah was going to abandon the safety of her bedroom each night, then Jane wouldn't have to feel guilty for invading her niece's privacy. After all, she wouldn't be doing it if Dinah were sleeping in her bed right now.

Somewhere nearby, a fork of lightning struck earth, and Jane shuddered at the light and the boom. Storms hadn't bothered her in the past—but now, walking alone through this creaking home with all its dusty chambers, she wished the rain would surrender to a clear, calm night.

She switched on the lamp atop Dinah's nightstand and got on her knees to check under the bed. There, she found some dust bunnies, a lonely striped sock, an English textbook, and what appeared to be a white, stuffed bunny crammed between the bed frame and the wall. Overall, nothing suspicious there.

Jane stood. Surely, Dinah was up to *something*. She turned and saw Dinah's closet. Yes, the closet . . . a popular place for stashing things you'd rather not have your parents find, as Jane recalled from her own adolescence.

She walked across the room to the closet, but as she opened the bi-fold doors, more lightning flashed outside, and the houselights suddenly blacked out, leaving Jane all but blind.

Instinctively, she jumped and tucked her body against the wall for protection. There, in the darkness, she understood why Dinah found their home so eerie.

Luckily, Jane was a grown-up, and she'd thought ahead. There was a storm outside, and she was a woman alone in a big house, so she'd brought along a flashlight, one of the big, metal ones that she could use to fend off anything that jumped out at her—not that she believed that would ever happen, of course . . . but just in case.

In the pitch black of Dinah's room, Jane rummaged through hanger upon hanger of dresses, many of which Dinah had made for herself. The girl had talent, no doubt. Jane checked pockets of jackets and coats, turning up the occasional pen or mitten, but nothing out of the ordinary or dangerous.

But there *had* to be something. . . .

She checked shoeboxes and plastic bins filled with old dolls and stuffed animals. Nothing.

She stood on her tiptoes and reached her hands along the top shelf, feeling for small boxes or the like. But the shelf was bare.

Frustrated, Jane shoved the dresses back into position. But as she pointed the flashlight into the back of the closet, its light hit one of the far walls, and there she found something peculiar: a keyhole, hidden next to an old, exposed wooden beam.

How weird, Jane thought. The keyhole had been fashioned of metal, of course, but it had been painted over with the rest of the bedroom, making it harder to see.

Jane hadn't found any keys in the closet, which dispirited her until she came to realize that she couldn't find any hinges around the keyhole for a door, either. She shined the flashlight directly onto the wall, even ran her hands along the surface, yet she found nothing that would mark the compartment into which this keyhole gave access. So, much as it puzzled her, Jane decided the keyhole must be another strange quirk of the house, a mystery to be solved later. For now, though, she was confident that Dinah had very little to do with it, especially considering the paint lacked the kinds of scratches you'd expect to find if someone were using keys around it.

"Excuse me?" said a voice behind Jane. She jumped, hitting her head on the pole supporting all the hangers. It popped out of its hinge, and all the dresses came sliding down to the floor.

Jane turned, shining the flashlight—and found Dinah standing in the bedroom, near her window, holding a cup of yogurt.

"Dinah!" Aunt Jane shouted, embarrassed as she crawled out from the mess in the closet. "Where have you *been?*"

"Home," Dinah answered. "Getting a snack."

"No. I've been downstairs the whole time, except when I was looking for you upstairs."

"We have a big house." Dinah spooned some yogurt into her mouth. "Here's my proof. We must've just missed each other."

Aunt Jane didn't like this scene at all. For one, she looked quite the fool sneaking around in Dinah's room and collapsing her niece's wardrobe. Two, the whole house was out of power, and Jane didn't need to be startled by Dinah, of all people. *Dinah* was the one who was supposed to be scared all the time, even if she didn't look it right now.

Thunder grumbled outside. Jane had barely seen the lightning flickering on Dinah's wall.

Something was different about Dinah. Normally, she had two ways of acting in the house: either Dinah sulked, her eyelids half closed, her lips turned to frowning, or she was shaking in her bed, mouth agape in a silent scream from some unseen fright. Now, Dinah stood in an entirely different posture: She appeared ready, aware, and quite comfortable in the blacked-out house. The Dinah Jane knew would *never* have left her bed to get a snack in the middle of a night like this, unless it was to go traipsing off to who-knows-where. The Dinah she knew was a frightened creature; this young woman seemed of a different character entirely.

And it scared Aunt Jane.

"I don't know what you're up to," she said.

"Getting some calcium." Dinah took another spoonful of yogurt.

"How *dare* you be so flip about this!"

"About what?"

"You. Leaving this house. Not taking your meds. Panic-stricken at all hours of the night. And me at my—"

"I'm not panic-stricken," Dinah answered.

Her calm voice grated on Jane. What was this? Now Dinah had multiple personalities? It was too much. All too much. Whatever Dinah was up to, she wasn't going to reveal it, and Aunt Jane had reached the end of her tolerance. She'd tried to understand. She'd tried to keep Dinah safe, here at the house with her, as long as she could, despite Dr. Morstan's suggestions. But seeing her niece in the middle of the night, without hope of turning on the lights, yet finding comfort in the darkness, Jane finally lost it.

"I'm calling Dr. Morstan," she said. "Right now. I can't—I can't do this anymore."

"Why? What's happened?"

"You! You. I can't understand what's happening to you. Who you are. I've tried. I'm sorry."

Aunt Jane rushed to grab the wireless phone from her robe pocket—another smart move on her part—and she began to dial Dr. Morstan's pager. He'd told her she could call at any time, but she'd resisted the temptation until now.

She'd dialed the first three numbers by the time the lightning struck. A brilliant blue-white bolt came down so close to their yard, Jane thought she could feel her hair stand from the electricity. At once, the room was bright as if on fire, and the subsequent thunder—so close and loud, like a shotgun blast at the ear—shook the room and caused a hanging picture of Dinah and her parents to drop from its nail and bounce against the floorboards.

Jane fell from the shock of the light and crashing. She screamed and dropped the phone, which slid across the room to Dinah's feet. And as Jane looked up, she saw her niece standing there, still in the middle of the room, her outline sharp against the skyline.

Dinah hadn't moved. She hadn't screamed or jumped. She'd simply looked out the window, muttered something like, "Wow," and ate another spoonful of yogurt.

"Dinah," Jane whispered. "Are you okay?"

"Yes," Dinah answered. "Are you?"

Dinah walked to her aunt and helped her to her feet.

Jane looked down at the phone. The cover had popped off, and the battery dangled from the phone like animal guts. She could grab it, fix it, make the call, but . . .

But it was over. Her anxiety had passed. And she was tired.

"Will you go to sleep?" Aunt Jane asked.

"Sure," Dinah said. "I'll see you in the morning."

☽

Of course, she'd lied to Aunt Jane, or at least misled her. Dinah *would* be leaving home tonight, even if the storm never relented; she *would* travel with Vincent away from the safety of town, deep into the woods, until they reached the Sunken Mausoleum. There, they would join Edaniel and find the next soul who needed saving. Together, they'd do the job every night, until it was complete.

She hadn't asked for any of this. If Destiny had offered, Dinah would have requested that she not be orphaned, nor see ghosts, nor be bound to helping the restless find peace. But that proposal had never come. However senselessly, accidentally, or even maliciously, life had dealt her this hand, this fate. . . .

And from now on, Dinah Wherever intended to play it.

FAN FICTION

STORY BY EVA NOEL
BASED ON THE MANGA BY M. ALICE LeGROW

THE RISING

*I*t used to be the sewing that kept her sane. The steady flicker of the silvery needle in the moonlight was hypnotizing. She would place her dress form beside the window, letting her see out into the wide, supposedly empty sanitarium yard. (She found it far better to know exactly where *they* were.) Then, she would let her consciousness slide into the rhythms of needle and thread while her unconscious mind kept a wary eye open.

Dinah didn't need the sewing anymore, although it was still calming.

Her dress form, currently displaying a wine-colored jacket in the early stages of construction, was still by the window—but more to take advantage of the day's fading natural light than to placate her madness. And Dinah still knelt beside the form in deep contemplation—but less from a desire to shut out the world than a need to decide what to do with these horrible bone buttons.

Edrear had given them to her, the bone buttons—which was a very nice gesture, make no mistake. He'd made them himself, though he'd refused to tell Dinah from what sort of creature he'd taken the bone. The buttons were carved to resemble shining white wagon wheels. If they hadn't been so impossibly large and a bit ragged at the edges, they might've worked on a winter coat. But Dinah already had several winter coats, as well as a winter cape, a winter cloak, a winter wrap, and a winter hoodie. She'd briefly considered making some winter gear for Vincent, but she figured neither he nor Edrear would appreciate that use of the buttons.

There was nothing to be done. She would have to use the buttons on a jacket for herself. And wear it. In public.

Decision made, Dinah stretched, letting the buttons clink between her fingers. Maybe if she added some distracting embellishments, the gigantic buttons would be less noticeable. She crawled over to her scrap bag, digging around for something appropriate. Nothing. She would have to ask Aunt Jane to visit the fabric store in Watertown.

Aunt Jane was very accommodating on this account, but she had notoriously bad taste in lace. Hideous lace might be fitting in this case, but it would still be better if Dinah could go to the store herself. Then, she'd be able to run the trim through her hands, holding it up to the various colored fabrics in the store. Maybe she could go with Aunt Jane this time.

Dinah bit her lip. Watertown was so far away: thirty minutes if you took the highway. Dinah no longer feared ghosts and monsters; the Sunken Mausoleum had seen to that. But the stark blacktop of a four-lane highway still made Dinah shiver. The pine trees lining the highway hemmed her in, and the uncanny straightness of the road seemed to pointing her directly toward a violent collision. Again.

Maybe Aunt Jane could use back roads?

Dinah was spared further contemplation by a gentle rapping at her window. Night had fallen, and Vincent had come to accompany her to the Mausoleum. She had no time to think about lace or highways. There was a job to do.

Charity
Have Charity, good friend,
And hear my tale to its end.
Three young siblings, all in a row,
Sent by Death, in the ground they did go.
The first was Bitterness, for full twenty years.
The second is she who tries to lie here.
The final was Fortunate, for before he dies,
From the bare earth, his sister does rise.

"Well," said Edaniel, "*someone* likes their superfluous capital letters."

Capitalized words were the only thing superfluous about this grave, Dinah mused. Tonight's vault was remarkable only in its plainness when compared to the others she, Vincent, Edaniel, and Edrear had opened since these nightmarish tasks began. There were no statues, no elaborate carvings, not even an inscription on the tomb other than the rhyme, simply a gray box, about six feet long, which only came up to Dinah's knees. The grave was a monument to stark nothingness, as if it hoped to erase all traces of whoever was inside.

"I'm not really sure where to start," Dinah said, bending down to run her fingers along the riddle plaque.

"Let's get it open," suggested Vincent. "Maybe there's more than meets the eye."

"Yeah," said Edaniel, "if we hit the right switch, maybe it'll transform into a car."

Dinah, Vincent, and Edrear knelt down for better leverage, but all they did was strain their muscles against the solid cover. They slumped down several minutes later, panting.

"C'mon, push, you ninnies!" scolded Edaniel.

"You could help, you know," Edrear said, wiping the sweat from his brow.

"Do I have to do everything myself?" asked Edaniel. *"Walla walla, Washington!"* he hollered. And with a swift kick from his pointy hind leg, Edaniel cracked the heavy cover straight across, causing one side to slide to the ground with a heavy thud.

Dinah and Vincent stared in shock.

Edrear interrupted the silence that, while not quite thick enough to require a knife to cut it, at least needed a fork wielded with a very persistent hand. "We loosened it for you," he said.

Vincent and Dinah alone were strong enough to push the remaining cracked slab aside, after which all four of them leaned over to peer into the tomb. Inside, in stark contrast to the barren exterior, was the most delicately carved statue Dinah had ever seen. This piece had never been weathered by the elements like most of the Sunken Mausoleum's statuary.

The statue was of a young woman, possibly in her late teenage years. Her face, carved of pinkish marble, seemed as if it would be soft to the touch. She was clothed in what looked to be a simple nightdress, but the folds of the stone fabric seemed to move and resettle as shadows wavered across the statue. The only thing marring the sculpture's beauty was the thick, wooden stake, which had been inserted where the girl's heart would be. Dinah felt an irrational urge to rip it out and hurl it away.

"That's . . . extremely odd," Edrear said.

"A stake through the heart," observed Vincent. "I don't like where this is going."

"Where is it going?" asked Edaniel. "As much as it pains me, I gotta agree with my brother: It's kinda weird."

"Vampires," said Vincent. "That's how you kill vampires."

"There are no such things as vampires," Edrear said disparagingly.

Dinah could hear the others talking, but all she could feel was a tightening spiral of wrong in her stomach. The statue looked so peaceful otherwise, but the wooden monstrosity stood in the way of the figure's serenity. Unable to take it anymore, Dinah wrenched the stake from the sculpture. Before she could toss the thing away, however, she heard an inauspicious click. The statue's upper body sprang up at the waist, so that it appeared to be sitting up. Dinah threw one arm over her face as she dropped the stake in shock as the others jumped away.

"See?" said Vincent. "I don't like this at all."

Collecting herself, Dinah joined the others inspecting the statue.

"Hey, check it out," said Edaniel, leaping onto the statue's upright head. "There's a ladder behind here. Let's climb into the coffin, everyone!"

As they descended, the smooth sepulchral walls turned to crumbling earth, then to damper, richer smelling soil, then to rough bark, and then to dense branches speckled with small chinks of light. Finally, Dinah and her friends found themselves climbing out of a large oak tree at the edge of Bizenghast Forest. The forest seemed smaller than usual to Dinah, but this was probably an illusion borne of the vast snow-covered farm fields that had become tree-covered in modern Bizenghast.

It was colder in the dream, probably mid-February to mid-March, but Dinah didn't mind. Whatever magic had brought them here also had provided her with a warm cape and mittens.

The sky was a sharp blue, and completely empty. Standing under the bare oak, looking up at the sky through the twisted branches, Dinah could almost see something beautiful about the forest—at least, until she took a step forward and her foot broke through the layer of ice covering about two feet of accumulated winter snow. "Ugh!" she cried.

"Careful, Miss Dinah," Edrear said, pulling her up by her arm. Vincent floundered over to help with her other arm, but Dinah was already precariously balanced on the snow's hard crust.

"Man," said Edaniel. "You guys really need to learn to redistribute your weight onto four legs. But don't worry. Just imagine the stories you'll get to tell your grandchildren: 'In my day, we walked two miles in the snow, uphill both ways, to free restless spirits! And we liked it!'"

Trudging through the snow to the main road was cold, wet work, and certainly not made easier by Edaniel skating figure eights around his heavier, less mobile companions. When they finally stumbled onto a wider thoroughfare, Dinah and Vincent shook out their clothes, whereas Edrear dusted off his armor.

"This must be Exeter Highway," said Vincent. "It was the only way into Bizenghast until the early twentieth century."

Following the highway was much easier traveling, and Dinah was able to pay attention to who was on the road with them. At first, there were only a few other people heading into town with them—a farm wagon with an entire family in the back that had rattled past without a passenger sparing them a single glance. As they grew closer to the village, though, they were accompanied by more and more men and women on the road, all obviously in a hurry. The faster the people around them went, the faster Dinah and the others felt they needed to go. Something was spurring everyone to Bizenghast, and they couldn't miss whatever it was.

Finally, the four gathered under the eaves of a building at the edge of the town green, watching what seemed like the entire county gather in the square.

"What's going on?" Dinah wondered.

"I could sneak in and check it out," Edaniel suggested.

"Don't you think you're a little conspicuous?" asked Vincent.

"Nonsense! I'll wear my reconnaissance hat. No one will suspect," said Edaniel.

His reconnaissance hat turned out to be small brimmed, with two large ostrich plumes, a badly tied blue bow, and a stuffed tanager perched in the center.

"What?" asked Edaniel, offended at their stares. "They're Victorians. They won't notice a thing."

Edaniel slunk toward the ever-increasing crowd, the front of his hat pushing up snow like a plough. He made a few loop-de-loops, and finally disappeared between the legs of some people gathered in front of a huge, unfinished construction project at the far side of the town square.

Studying the scene for a moment, Dinah quickly worked out that the building would one day become the library.

"Perhaps you should provide my brother with some cover, Master Vincent," Edrear said a moment or two after Edaniel had vanished from sight. "Miss Dinah and I will flank this crowd on the left. This will assure us maximum coverage."

"What?" asked Vincent, turning just in time to watch Edrear take Dinah's hand firmly and lead her away. "Oh, drat."

Dinah, for her part, stumbled gamely behind Edrear as he led her around the crowd. At another corner of the square, they crouched behind several barrels and tried to take stock of the scene. Dinah was not sure what they were trying to accomplish, moving all the way over here. They weren't any closer to the crowd. She could see a trio of ladies discussing something very seriously, but for all she could hear, they were talking about rhubarb and marmalade.

"Miss Dinah," said Edrear from behind her, "I hope you don't think that I was too bold in presenting you with those gifts last time we met."

Suddenly, Dinah's stomach dropped, her blush rose, and everything in between was stretched too thin. "No," she said, trying to decide if this warranted turning around. "No, not at all. I appreciate the thought, Edrear."

"I could . . ." Edrear fell silent, and Dinah suddenly wished she had turned around. It was very awkward listening to someone have a heartfelt pause behind one's back. She strained forward around a barrel, pretending she had seen something interesting. Edrear finally picked up his thoughts and continued: "I would be happy to make you more if you like."

"No!" Dinah said, perhaps a little more sharply than an offer of buttons deserved—but she had visions of the bulky, unattractive clothing that buttons from Edrear would demand. "No," she said, finally turning around to present a calmer face. "That's really not necessary."

Facing him had been a mistake. Edrear looked so serious, and Dinah was caught halfway between wanting to giggle at his face and the need to look equally serious.

He was suddenly holding her hand, and—

"You have to nip these things in the bud, Dinah." Edaniel leapt suddenly to her shoulder. "Watch this: Hey, Edrear. What. Is. Love?"

Edrear looked confused. "Huh?"

"See," said Edaniel, "he can usually go on and on like that, but if you present him with a conundrum of the human condition, his sophisticated robot brain just shuts down."

"I'm not a robot," argued Edrear.

"That's exactly what a robot *would* say," replied Edaniel.

"What did you find out?" asked Vincent, coming over to complete the thorough interruption of Edrear's cunning plan.

"Brief synopsis," said Edaniel: "A suicidally depressed man goes to sea, discovers his captain has lost his freaking mind, chases a white whale and . . .wait, no. That's *Moby-Dick*. What's going on *here* is this: Two years ago, a young woman died a slow, withering death. Two months ago, her younger sister died the exact same way. Right now, their brother is suffering from the same symptoms."

"'Three young siblings,'" quoted Dinah. "How terrible."

"Uh-huh. Their father is convinced he knows the source of the problem."

"A tainted well?" asked Edrear.

"No, a vampire."

"Told you!" shouted an exasperated Vincent.

"It isn't actually a vampire, is it?" asked Dinah.

"Of course it isn't. Like Edrear said, there are no such things as vampires. The father, however, does not have the benefit of our wisdom. He thinks that the daughter who just died is rising from the grave and feeding on her brother. He's gathering a posse right now to take care of it."

"What does that mean?" asked Vincent.

"I dunno, Chauncey. Maybe we should follow the now-absent crowd and find out."

Dinah looked around, shocked, to find the town square was empty of everyone except a few lingering ladies. "Where did they go?"

"Lucky you have me here to pay attention to the actual ghost, and not just to your training for the upcoming tri-angst-a-thon," said Edaniel. "They're going to the Browns'. If we hurry, we'll probably catch them before old man Brown starts speechifying about the devil."

They ran, following the trail of tramped down snow and slick, brown mud patches left by the passing of many people. Twilight was falling when Dinah and the others caught up to the crowd approaching a colonial farmhouse. They were caught up in a column of men, many carrying unlit torches, several with pitchforks, and a few with rifles. This was no medieval mob, Dinah realized.

"Maybe you should stay back, Dinah," whispered Vincent.

"What are you talking about?" she asked.

"Look around. All the women have disappeared. They're not going to talk about whatever it is they're going to do if delicate ears are going to hear them."

"I don't have delicate ears! I want to be a part of this, Vincent."

"I didn't say you did!" protested Vincent. "And I didn't say you couldn't!"

"Oh, fine!" snapped Dinah. "They can't see Edaniel's ridiculous hat, but they can see a girl?"

"Hey," said Edaniel, "I like that hat."

"I'm just saying—" started Vincent.

"To stay out of your way?"

"Don't listen to them," Edaniel said to his hat. "You're still beautiful to me."

"We can investigate this without you," said Vincent.

Dinah sighed, exasperated, spinning away and marching off into the field without another word.

"What did I do?" appealed Vincent to Edrear and Edaniel

Edrear shrugged. "I do not understand women."

"That's 'cause you weren't programmed with that algorithm," replied Edaniel.

Dinah had to admit she was glad it had gotten dark so quickly. She had impressed herself with her graceful flounce away from Vincent, but as soon as she was ten feet from the worn path, the snow had gotten deep and difficult to maneuver again. It was far less satisfying to wallow away from someone after a fight.

She went wide around the Browns' home, watching briefly as the group of men gathered in front of the house, lighting their torches. Okay, maybe she couldn't hear what they were saying. There was no reason she couldn't do a little looking around. Maybe the boys would get their information their own way, but she might find something to add all by herself.

It was darker at the back of the house; Dinah's eyes took a minute to adjust. Soft light spilled out of one of the windows, and Dinah crept forward to investigate. The shadows would hide her from whoever was inside as long as she stayed out of the light. She blinked, trying to get a grasp on where she should stand. There was a splotch on her retina that would not fade, a patch of darkness with no depth. Dinah headed for it, knowing that when she had more light, it would go away.

And then it moved.

Dinah bit back her scream with a grinding of teeth she knew would make her jaw ache the next day. This was no time for theatrics. Dinah resolutely stepped forward, waiting for the shadow to move again or for the window's light to make it clear. The shadow stepped into the light. It was only a girl.

Dinah froze. "Charity?" she guessed.

The girl looked older than the statue in the graveyard, but it was impossible to tell how old someone carved of marble was. This living face was ruddy, and her eyes were bugging out of her head. She was pulling on her long, brown hair desperately. Her chest rose and fell heavily, and her jaw worked as if she was gasping, but Dinah couldn't hear any breath pass her lips.

"Are you Charity?" Dinah asked again.

The girl groaned and put her hands over her face. Dinah stumbled forward to help, or to comfort, or to try something. The girl groaned again as Dinah took her shoulders and pulled her close. And then the smell hit: dry and musty like the grave they had climbed into. Dinah didn't let go, but she pulled her face away. "Charity?" she whispered.

The girl looked into Dinah's face and bared her teeth—her sharp, pure white teeth. There was a strangled cry, which Dinah would later determine had been her own. She fully expected a bite, but there was only a solid pain in her mid-section as the girl shoved her into the side of the house. She hit the ground with a muffled thud and lay still for a moment, pulling herself together and watching for moving shadows.

So much for "no such things as vampires."

As nothing happened for the next few moments, and lying in the snow was rapidly making her wet and uncomfortable, Dinah pulled herself back to her feet. The light from the window hadn't even wavered. Anyone inside probably hadn't noticed the ruckus outside. Deciding that not checking would be a waste of a perfectly painful collision with a house, Dinah peered in through the window. She looked in on a bedroom, but the head of the bed was angled away from the window, hiding the occupant. Pressing her face against the glass, she could just make out an arm flopped across a quilt.

The window had no lock, nor a screen, so it wouldn't be too difficult to open it and climb in the room. Getting her fingernails under the sash, Dinah paused. Everyone thought there was a vampire on the loose. Hell, there *was* a vampire on the loose. Breaking and entering was probably not the safest occupation at the moment.

With a deep breath, Dinah wrenched open the window. The cold had numbed her fingers enough that there was only a twinge under her nails, but she knew her hands would ache tomorrow. Hauling herself over the sill, Dinah got her first look at the inside of the house. It was remarkably plain, with empty walls and minimal furniture, but it wasn't as if she were there to critique the décor. A sudden burst of coughing attracted her attention to the bed she had seen from the window. In it was a boy no older than ten.

He looked terrible. His skin was sallow and his eyes were dark-ringed. His hair was lank with the sweat that beaded on his forehead and ran down his jaw as Dinah watched. Dinah approached cautiously, but he couldn't see her through his blurred, half-lidded eyes. She touched his burning face; his fever was soaring. Turning his head to the side, she pulled away his hair and found . . . nothing. Not a single mark.

She checked the other side, but found the skin equally unblemished. Leaning with one hand against the open window, Dinah closed her eyes to think. Sudden shouting pulled her up short. The men at the front of the house were on the move. She had to get out of there.

Coming back to the front of the house, Dinah hoped that Vincent and the others had actually bothered to wait for her. Peering cautiously around the corner, she found that all the men had gone. There was nobody around that she could see. She felt a sudden urge to stomp her feet or swear up a blue streak.

"Psssst," said a voice near her feet, "the eagle lands at 3:15, Mountain time."

"Edaniel?" asked Dinah, all the while berating herself for sounding like an idiot, because who else could it be down there?

"Dinah!" called Vincent, and suddenly he and Edrear were bursting out of the darkness. "Where have you been?"

"Around," Dinah said coolly, not quite ready to share what she had learned.

"It's good you found us when you did, Miss Dinah," said Edrear. "We have to steal Charity Brown's body right away."

"I keep telling you," said Vincent, "that's not going help the perception that she's a vampire!"

"She's already dead. I don't think she cares what they think," replied Edrear, "We're here to prevent the desecration of her body! Farmer Brown and the village men have gone to the chapel to be blessed by the pastor. Miss Dinah, they're going to go to exhume Charity Brown on the pretense that she's a vampire."

"Well," said Dinah, "she is."

"Excuse me?" The words seemed to come from all directions at once; Dinah was uncertain which of them had actually said it.

Edrear opened his mouth to scoff, but Dinah cut him off, "I saw it myself. I saw her brother, too, in the house. I think he has tuberculosis."

"That's Edgar Brown," Edaniel informed her. "You're probably right."

"Wait, time out," said Vincent. "A vampire is killing Edgar?"

"No, no," said Edaniel. "Pay attention. He died of consumption."

"But she saw a vampire!"

"It's entirely possible there's a vampire, too," said Edaniel. "Doesn't mean it's actually killing him. Did I forget to mention that?"

"You might have missed it," Vincent replied sarcastically. "In fact, you said there were no such things as vampires."

"Yeah, in the real world," replied Edaniel. "But that doesn't mean a ghost can't dream one up."

"So, if Edgar Brown really died of tuberculosis," began Vincent, "this is just an, I don't know, *incidental* vampire?"

"It happens," said Edaniel defensively. "You know how it is. You buy the house in February, thinking everything's fine, but then the summer months come along and—*Wham!*—your house is infested with them."

"What?" asked Dinah, who had never heard of this particular home-ownership problem.

"It doesn't matter where the vampire—if it even is one—came from," interjected Edrear. "We should still go collect her body, dead or undead! If the villagers get it first, Edgar will be dead no matter what we do."

"Why?" asked Dinah.

"They're going to grind up her heart and feed it to her brother as a cure," explained Vincent.

"And as a licensed medical professional," said Edaniel, "I can tell you that ain't gonna work."

"If Charity is a vampire," said Edrear, "we'll put her to rest ourselves and save the boy in the process."

"How?" demanded Vincent.

"The usual way," said Edrear, shaking his head at Vincent's stupidity. "We raid her lair while she sleeps, put a stake through her heart, chop off her head, stuff it with garlic, and set the whole mess on fire."

"So, not complicated at all," Vincent said. "You sure know a lot about the disposal of creatures you repeatedly claimed didn't exist."

Edrear took a defensive step toward Vincent, but he didn't flinch. "If you would just drop the sarcasm, this would be easier," snapped Edrear.

"You know what would make this a whole lot easier?" returned Vincent. "If you and your brother would actually give us the information necessary to our job."

"Hey," said a nervous Edaniel, "don't drag me into this pissing contest, okay? I can't do it standing up."

Vincent snorted and glared at Edrear. "Furthermore—"

"That's enough!" snapped Dinah. "We don't have time for this!"

Both boys mumbled their apologies, but they continued to glare at each other as Dinah outlined her plan.

"I agree with Edrear. We just have to get Charity out of her father's way. If she's dead, she's dead. If she's not—well, we can take an ax from the Brown's woodpile if she puts up a fight," she said, "and I'm sure I could sneak into their pantry to steal some garlic. I've already broken into the house once tonight."

Her second trip into the house was far less eventful than the first. Armed with sharp instruments and several garlic bulbs, Dinah and the others hurried to the Bizenghast cemetery. They fanned out between the graves to search for Charity's tomb, eyes and ears open for the first sign of farmer Brown and his men returning from the church. "It's kind of weird," said Vincent, "that we've ended up in a graveyard inside a ghost's dream. It's like a play within a play, but with dead people."

"Hey, folks!" called Edaniel from a far corner of the graveyard. "Quit talking about narrative devices and get over here! I found Charity."

Her gravestone here was much the same as the one at the Sunken Mausoleum. Without the puzzle plaque, the cover of the sarcophagus was even plainer, with only her name and the date of her death.

Dinah knelt beside it and ran a finger along the seal. "That's odd," she said. "It doesn't appear to be broken."

"Let's get it open," suggested Edrear, picking up the ax.

"Don't smash it!" cried Dinah.

"We're already robbing her grave," said Vincent reasonably. "It's a bit late for delicacy."

Holding it high over his head, Edrear forcefully brought the ax down on the grave slab. Despite being nearly new, he shattered the stone to pieces with three quick strokes. Dinah and Vincent pulled away the largest pieces, tossing them into the woods surrounding the cemetery.

Edaniel climbed to the head of the grave, looked in, and whistled low. "No wonder they thought she was a vampire, guys. She looks alive!"

"She *is* a vampire," Vincent said crossly, hauling away a particularly large piece of stone.

Dinah joined Edaniel at the grave, brushing debris off the rosy cheeks and calm expression of the body inside. Charity did, in fact, look as if she would open her eyes and ask what was for breakfast at any moment. "She's not the vampire," said Dinah.

"What?" came the chorus of voices again.

"Dinah," said Vincent, "you said earlier—"

"I was wrong. This girl is younger than the one I saw."

"Maybe that's just the effect of lying still," said Edrear. "People often look younger in their sleep. Or death."

"Also, she's blonde."

"Maybe she stopped at the salon for a wash and dye before returning to her grave?" suggested Edaniel gamely. "Just because you're dead doesn't mean you should stop looking fabulous."

Dinah sat on the raised grave beside Charity's and held her head in her hands. When would things start making sense? They could save Charity's brother from the marvels of "modern" medicine, but that didn't explain what she had seen at the Brown's farmhouse. If they couldn't find the vampire, would it even matter? Did it actually have anything to do with the dream, or was it just a red herring? Dinah pounded her fist on the rough stone, flinching when she scraped a bit of skin off her hand. Pulling up sharply, she finally noticed whose grave she was sitting on: Miriam Brown.

"Bitterness," she said.

"Yeah, now is not a good time for random association theatre," said Edaniel. "The rest of us are still in the process of stealing a corpse, so any time you want to jump in on that—"

"No," said Dinah. "The older sister. Miriam means 'bitterness.' That's what all the capital letters were in the riddle: names. Miriam, Charity . . . and I'm willing to bet Edgar means 'Fortunate.'"

"There's Death, too," Vincent reminded Dinah.

"Death is the biggest name in the business," said Edaniel.

Dinah continued, "The poem didn't say Charity rose from

the grave, just 'his sister.' What if we're after the wrong sister?"

"I have an ax," said Edrear, "and we have another coffin to smash. I say we find out exactly who's walking around—"

"Edrear," interrupted Edaniel, "have you sprung a leak?"

"What sort of question is that?"

"Well, *someone* is losing air. You hear that sound?"

Dinah hadn't heard it before, but she could certainly hear it now that Edaniel had pointed it out. It was a low, steady hissing, like steam escaping from a manhole cover. In the dark, she couldn't tell from what direction it came.

She and the boys formed a circle, back to back, keeping their eyes open.

Miriam was no more than ten feet away before they could see her. She looked sick and bloated, but very much alive. Her jaw hung open as if she couldn't close it, and the air hissed out her mouth, hot and angry.

Spotting them at her sister's grave, the walking corpse's mouth snapped shut—and in the sudden silence, Dinah heard another noise: rocks, rolling down a hill, or else rubble, shifting off a moving body in a grave.

"Uh-oh," said Edaniel, "our mystery guest is about to sign in."

Dinah didn't want to look at Charity's grave. Their situation was becoming exponentially worse. It wasn't fair for a puzzle to say "sister" when it really meant "sisters." Plurals were very important, especially when one was being surrounded. Especially when one was being surrounded by beings that didn't even—

"Edrear, I think you need to explain to these ladies that they don't exist," said Dinah.

There was a dizzyingly long moment when everyone was looking at her, even the vampire, in open-mouthed confusion, and Dinah felt like the biggest idiot who had ever tried to will something into nonexistence. Even the shifting rocks behind her stopped briefly. But really, being threatened by undead creatures in a nightmare of the past was no time for grade-school level embarrassment. Dinah believed she had a fairly good grasp of the situation, and she needed to make this clear to everyone else. "They weren't vampires."

"I don't think that's a very convincing argument at the moment," said Vincent.

As if in agreement, Miriam lurched forward and bared her teeth at them.

"No, it's the perfect argument." Dinah turned around and faced Charity's grave. She could see the girl's facial muscles twitching, as if in a bad dream. "Your sister wasn't a vampire, Charity. And you didn't turn into one, either. It doesn't matter what you heard before you died."

Miriam made a guttural sound and dove toward Dinah. Edrear cut her off with a swing of the ax, and the vampire arched away. Her face was redder than ever, and contorted with fury.

Dinah knelt beside the grave and tried to trust that the others would watch her back. "I need you to believe me," she said to Charity.

Behind her, Vincent had tackled Miriam to the ground. "Hold her still," said Edrear, readying the ax. He took a swing, but Miriam gouged her fingernails into Vincent's arm and twisted away before the ax struck.

"Would you please not swing that around while I'm in the way?" shouted Vincent.

"Sorry," muttered Edrear, not really sounding all that sorry.

Dinah had reached an impasse with Charity. The sounds of Miriam hissing and snarling at Edrear and Vincent had sped up Charity's transformation. The ghost's eyelashes were fluttering, and her lips were drawing back from her teeth. Dinah knew it was unfair for her to be upset that someone actively turning into a vampire didn't believe her when she said there were no vampires, but she wanted to scream at Charity for buying so easily into the lie. "You're not to blame," Dinah said hopelessly. "No matter what you were told."

Charity had believed people like her father, who had told her that her sister was to blame for her disease, and that she would be responsible for her brother's sickness. There was no way Dinah could compete with that kind of authority, especially considering she wasn't entirely sure she believed herself. She needed someone far more assertive—

"This sort of thing happens," said Edrear in between swings at the vampire, "because you humans encourage the *dumbest* fantasies!"

"I don't know," said Vincent. "It seems pretty plausible to me. I mean, ghosts are real, so why not vampires?"

"Next you will tell me you believe in Bigfoot!" snapped Edrear.

"Some of my best friends have big feet," said Edaniel.

"Do you all believe every bit of nonsense you hear?" shouted Edrear, dropping his ax to throw his arms up in the air. "There are no such things as vampires!"

Nothing happened for a second after he spoke, but when the echo of his voice finally stopped bouncing off the trees, Miriam took a step forward and promptly collapsed to the ground.

Edrear knelt beside the body, turning it over. She was finally at rest.

"Okay, Edrear," said Edaniel, "now say that Rodgers and Hammerstein musicals don't exist!"

Dinah had only a moment to sigh in relief before flickering torches appeared across the graveyard. "Cheese it!" hissed Edaniel. "It's the fuzz!"

There were a few frantic moments as Dinah realized they now had two bodies to carry off rather than one. Edrear hefted Miriam's larger body over his shoulders as Dinah and Vincent yanked Charity's body fully out of her coffin. The girl was smaller than her sister, but still dead weight. Dinah held the corpse under her arms, while Vincent took the legs. The lights grew closer, and Dinah could hear the crowd of men talking softly to each other.

"C'mon!" hissed Edaniel, who was disappearing into the woods.

Dinah had never moved a body before, and she was surprised at how ridiculously difficult it was.

Vincent was hurrying backward, trying to avoid trees and keep up with Edrear and Edaniel. Dinah attempted to move as fast as him, but the body was so heavy, and it kept twisting whenever Vincent had to take a side step to avoid bramble. She could feel her grip slipping, but the furious shouts behind them in the forest convinced her that farmer Brown and the others had discovered the smashed-open tomb.

"What . . . about . . . Edgar?" gasped Vincent.

"He's got a better chance of survival now that he's not going to be feasting on his char-grilled heart of sister," said Edaniel.

They'd been running for five minutes more when Vincent, running ahead of Dinah, suddenly pitched forward and disappeared from her line of sight. She had only a moment to wonder what had happened when the ground disappeared from beneath her own feet. She tumbled, head over heels over the accompanying corpse, down a stream bank she couldn't have seen in the darkness. As she rolled, she heard Edrear call her name and start to slide down the bank after her. She'd had time to think that stream banks weren't usually this deep when she came to a sudden stop and found herself sprawled out at the base of a centaur statue, leaves and sticks poking out of her hair and Vincent's elbow buried in her back.

They had made it back to the Sunken Mausoleum.

"Huh," said Edaniel, gracefully sliding into her tilted perspective. "I think we lost 'em."

The sun was rising in pinks and pale oranges as Dinah and Vincent arrived back at Dinah's window. "Ugh," said Vincent.

"I feel like we ran ten miles tonight. Maybe I should try out for track, put all these nights' work to use."

Dinah smiled as he handed her up through her window. "Good thing Edrear is so authoritative on the subject of vampires," she said. "I don't think I'm quite believable enough, especially when they're hissing in my face."

Vincent was looking at her strangely now, not moving away from the window, not saying goodbye as he usually did. Reaching for Dinah's hand, he said, "If you'd like, I could make you some buttons, too."

"Vincent—" started Dinah.

"And much nicer than those dinner plates Edrear made."

"It really isn't—"

"I haven't done much carving recently, but—"

"Vincent!" interrupted Dinah, taking both his hands in hers and looking him straight in the eye. "Believe me when I say, with perfect honesty, that there is nothing I would like *less* than to receive more buttons. You've been with me every night since the beginning. Nothing you could carve, weld, or knit me could ever equal that."

Vincent was satisfied with this response, or at least he appeared to be, mused Dinah as she flopped onto her bed. She didn't want to think about this now. She had only a few hours to sleep before she had to get up to accompany Aunt Jane to Watertown.

Dinah buried her face into her pillow and groaned. Who knew buttons could cause so much trouble? Exhaustion, ugly jackets, weirdness with Vincent, and, of course, driving . . .

Climbing under the covers, Dinah began to measure distances in her head. She faced death and dismemberment every night. Why was she so afraid of a little trip? Danger was just a question of what you believed.

Maybe she would ask Aunt Jane to take the highway.